Praise for

I0541485

A.J. Llewellyn and Serena Yates

A wonderful paranormal story... It's well written, has good descriptions, and a complicated mystery plot that kept me guessing...great sizzling hot sex...
~ *Literary Nymphs Reviews*

Creating a story takes a lot effort, especially if it's enticing, has interesting characters, beautiful scenery, and an enjoyable, well written plot. But a story which incorporates all of these qualities, while intricately entwining several layers which blend together and hold your attention and are understandable, is even more of an accomplishment...a passionate love story... Thanks AJ and Serena for a terrific reading experience. ~ *Queer Magazine Online*

Oh my God, this is a fantastic paranormal; magic, sexy men and an incredible cupcake story... This story has more twists and turns than a roller coaster, more ups and downs than a yo-yo and some surprising unexpected laughter...I am going to recommend this to everyone.
~ *MM Good Book Reviews*

Total-E-Bound Publishing books by A.J. Llewellyn and Serena Yates:

Elemental Superpowers
The Cake
The Blancmange

Elemental Superpowers

THE BLANCMANGE

A.J LLEWELLYN and
SERENA YATES

The Blancmange
ISBN # 978-0-85715-770-6
©Copyright A.J. Llewellyn and Serena Yates 2011
Cover Art by Posh Gosh ©Copyright 2011
Interior text design by Claire Siemaszkiewicz
Total-E-Bound Publishing

Published in 2012 by Total-E-Bound Publishing, Think Tank, Ruston Way, Lincoln, LN6 7FL, United Kingdom.

THE
BLANCMANGE

Dedication

To those who — like us — believe that dessert
should always be eaten first

Chapter One

Finn Garrison stepped out onto the sand and stretched. At six-foot-four, he was a big man and being scrunched up in a jury box day after day took its toll on him. Even his toes were happy to be back at the beach. He luxuriated in the chilly morning air and stared up at the sky.

He studied the appealing mix of shades. Brilliant blue with streaks of egg white cloud, a hint of green and soft grey. A whisper of rose. So much better than where he'd been. It reminded him of a Dairy Queen Blizzard. Why did he always think about things in terms of ice cream?

He longed to saunter over to Christopher's house, which was just three doors down, and start his morning with a cup of coffee. Christopher was so much fun and always lifted his spirits, but he could tell by their closed patio door that Christopher's lover, Marcel, was still home.

When Christopher was alone, music and good baking smells poured out of the open doors. That's how he and Christopher had first met—on the beach, discussing food. He gulped as he realised Marcel was not Finn's biggest fan. For some reason, he seemed jealous of the budding friendship between Christopher and Finn—which was ridiculous. Marcel was older, but the Fire Court judge had Christopher's heart. Finn was more like his...court jester.

He found himself wondering, not for the first time, about Christopher's relationship with the dangerous and powerful Marcel Paradis. They both held high positions in the Fire Council. They were part of the clandestine network of the super-secret elemental superpowers. So was Finn. Sometimes it made him feel like Batman, other times he felt like a lunatic.

If he told any regular person what his life was like, he'd wind up in a rubber room. A juror for the Water Court, Finn was adjudicating a difficult trial right now. Being new to the Northern California beach community of Half Moon Bay—his temporary home— he'd been relieved to meet Christopher and Marcel.

It had been a fluke really, since most people involved in elemental superpowers usually didn't fraternise outside of their special elemental zone. Christopher was different, though. He had friends in all of the houses—earth, air, fire and water.

Dang...maybe I do like him as more than a friend.

This thought worried him. Hankering for the wrong guy had already landed him in a whole world of hurt. He could just quietly walk by their house. Christopher wouldn't even need to know Finn was on the beach.

But I want him to see me. I want to hang out with him. I think he's seriously special. He's not only the hottest guy I've ever met, but nobody cooks the way he does.

Finn tried not to allow his romantic and sexual fantasies to filter into his brain. He had enough on his plate.

Still, he wavered. He longed to talk to Christopher, who was not only sympathetic and understanding, but also made a fantastic cup of coffee. Not that he'd discuss the actual case with the man—or more appropriately in Christopher's case, Mage—but Christopher could make sense of even the smallest peculiarities. He was a magic man. Finn had no idea what the guy put in the coffee he made, but it always left Finn feeling very mellow. Christopher Fire ran an incredible bakery called Fabulous Cupcakes with Marcel's son, Daine. It had become the hottest bakery in San Francisco, both with humans and the 'elementals'—as some people with superpowers called themselves.

In fact, Fabulous Cupcakes had become a kind of informal meeting place for all the superpowers. For the first time in centuries, the members had started congregating on neutral ground...there at the shop. The human customers had no idea what the hell was going on right under their noses, which was kind of fun.

But I go to that bakery just to see him. Oh, crap. I do like him, maybe more than I should. Fuckity fuckity fuck fuck fuck.

He stretched again, every muscle in his back and legs aching. The Kennedy trial should have been a routine murder trial but it had turned out to be nasty and very, very complicated. He yawned. Maybe he could stop by for a small cup of coffee and try extra hard to laugh at Marcel's jokes. He bit his lip, trying to strike up the courage. Something stopped him. The image of Marcel frowning came to mind.

Finn had never actually seen Marcel do anything mean but he'd heard stories about the mercurial judge setting fire to talkative courtroom watchers' hair. He'd given people hot feet and hot flashes. So Finn was always nice to the guy. He was aware that he, too, had powers and water could put out fire, but still…there was something frightening about Marcel.

Okay, so maybe I should stay away. I just got a nice haircut. Flames wouldn't improve it at all.

Finn blew out a breath and began to run along the foamy shoreline, passing Christopher's house, which was so near, and yet so far from his own beach bungalow.

A huge wave crashed to his left, startling him. Water sprayed him from nowhere, almost completely covering him, but his attention and body were diverted by Christopher, who'd come out of his house, waving frantically.

"Come and have breakfast. I tried calling you!"

Finn tripped over his own big feet in his haste to get to the house.

"Wow, you're all wet," Christopher said, handing him a fluffy blue towel. The man looked gorgeous. Wearing faded pale blue jeans the exact colour of his eyes and a white silk shirt, his tousled blond hair and ten-thousand kilowatt smile gave him the appearance of a supermodel. He was mesmerising.

"I just got decked by a huge wave," Finn replied.

"Really?" Christopher's brows knitted in a curious way.

Oh, I want to kiss that spot between his eyes. I want to undo each button and lick my way down his torso until I reach his treasure trail.

Stop, idiot. He's taken.

"But the water's so flat today." Christopher's nose crinkled as he looked past Finn's shoulder out towards the sea.

Finn turned. He was right. But the wave had been there, coming out of nowhere. Finn brushed the thought aside. Half Moon Bay, just thirty minutes south of San Francisco, was a picturesque, secluded enclave, but it was also a super-secret big wave spot. Swells just popped up out of seemingly harmless ripples. Surfer Mark Foo had drowned here several years ago and people still talked about it like it happened yesterday.

The smell of warm peach and lemon had him towel-drying himself in record time. He walked into the house, nodding to Marcel who sat on a high stool at the kitchen breakfast bar, in jeans and a mulberry coloured sweater, reading the morning paper. Finn knew that Christopher had knitted it. It had taken him ages. A lot of love had gone into it. The thought depressed Finn. He brought his thoughts back to the present.

"Good morning, Marcel," he said, putting a smile on his face.

It surprised Finn to see that the great, distinguished jurist was reading a human newspaper, but then again, nothing about Marcel was…well, normal.

"What's good about it?" Marcel glowered at him.

Maybe I should have sprayed my hair with fire retardant before I came over here…

"Well," Finn said, without thinking, "I have no jury duty today. It's such a relief. This trial is killing me, I swear."

For a moment, desolation gripped him. He hated the trial. *Hated* that he'd been summoned from his lonely, but very comfortable existence back in Mermaid

Beach, Bermuda, to sit in on the case. The powers-that-be had promised him it would take a week. He should have smelt a water rat when they'd offered to spring for accommodation.

He narrowed his eyes now. It was Saturday. On Monday, he and the other Water Court jurors would be embarking on their second month of witness testimony in what some had dubbed the 'Camelot' case.

As if reading his mind, Marcel glanced at him. "You're working the Camelot trial?" He carefully folded up his newspaper, placed it by his left elbow then leaned on the breakfast bar, staring at him. For the first time since they'd met, Marcel seemed to be interested in Finn.

Finn saw the crackle of fire cross Marcel's pupils. He wished he had a glass of water handy just in case he'd need to extinguish a fire on his crotch or something.

"Take a seat." Marcel held out the stool beside him.

Christopher beamed and put two bread plates and a basket of what Christopher called breakfast cupcakes between the two men. Finn called these delicacies godsends. He'd never tasted such fantastic cupcakes in his life. Christopher slid silverware beside them, then — to Finn's relief — poured him a cup of coffee. Finn took a seat, drinking from his cup the second Christopher stopped adding cream to it. He felt better, as if somehow Christopher had reached inside him and ironed out the spiritual kinks. Not that he would ever voice these thoughts aloud.

To anybody.

"So," Marcel purred. "You must tell me. Have you seen Mr. Kennedy yet?"

Finn hesitated. This was such a loaded question and he was afraid to answer it. He knew that the Water

Court had struggled to fill the jury seats for what had turned out to be anything but a routine case. It was bizarre. Strange things had happened to several prospective jurors and the case itself was...beyond weird. He longed to talk about it but knew it would violate all kinds of laws. He'd been concerned when they'd finally secured a working jury, then suddenly one member vanished. She'd been quickly replaced...well, a week later. But between the jury selection and the strange defendant himself, it hadn't been an easy case to handle.

A second juror had been injured in a hit and run accident. He'd been knocked down by a human, but it had rattled the entire jury. The man's unfortunate accident meant that the jury had been given the weekend off. It had been Finn's first day off in two months. Superpowers courts didn't work like human ones. Their trials went on every single day until the matter was settled. Nobody had ever seen a case like this.

He realised suddenly that it may take months to settle. He'd be stuck in the courtroom forever if the defence had their way. He was nervous and tired. He longed for advice...for sympathy. He couldn't talk to anybody and it made him feel like he was heading for a breakdown.

Finn felt that—as much as he envied Marcel's relationship with Christopher—he could trust the man, but...well...*did* he trust him? And *should* he?

He held his cup in one hand, surreptitiously draping the other hand across his lap. It didn't offer his crotch much protection but it was better than nothing should Marcel harbour a desire to firebomb him.

The second sip of coffee was as good as the first. The fog in his brain started to lift and he was certain he could come up with a snappy answer that would satisfy Marcel's curiosity, keep him interested in having a conversation with Finn, *and* convey the weighted truth that yes, he'd seen Kennedy.

Christopher held the glass coffee carafe in his hand and stared at Finn.

"My God...you've seen him," he whispered. He went to put the pot on the bar but clipped it against the edge, accidentally. The glass shattered, hot coffee flying everywhere, startling all three of them.

"Stay there." Marcel put a warm hand on Finn's arm. Heat soared through his body and he realised he couldn't move.

Christopher frantically cleaned up and, out of nowhere, produced a second, identical carafe.

"Fresh coffee, coming right up." He smiled. Finn tried to relax. Instead he found himself immobile and sweating. He'd heard about Marcel's fondness for using this power. It was most persuasive on hostile witnesses. Finn almost giggled.

I'd love to see him try this on Kennedy...

"This is a big case for Bainbridge, isn't it?" Marcel asked.

Nice one. He's trying to make me feel like we're equals. He's trying to get me to showboat, to spill everything I know.

Finn tried to take another sip of coffee, but his arm wouldn't cooperate. His desperate eyes sought Christopher's gaze.

Christopher stared right back and frowned.

"Darling, that's not nice. Unfreeze him immediately. Haven't I asked you not to paralyse our guests?"

Marcel harrumphed and suddenly Finn could move again. He gulped at his coffee. He wanted to get out of here.

He felt better now that he had control of his body again. His hand shook as he lifted the coffee cup to his lips.

Marcel seemed to be waiting. Tough. He could keep waiting. It irritated Finn that Marcel seemed to think that Finn was some child he could goad and control. He resisted the temptation to roll his eyes at the casual way Marcel had raised the topic of Ephyrus Bainbridge, he of the law firm of Arden, Bainbridge, Chinook and Damek. It was a large, Fortune 500 company that handled major criminal cases both in the human and the superpowers realms.

Ephyrus Bainbridge was the partner who oversaw the cases for the Water Court and personally handled the big ones. The Kennedy trial was as big as they came. Finn began to panic. The trial had distressed him more than he'd thought was possible. He saw danger in every conversation, conspiracy in every glance in his direction.

He drained his coffee fast, even though it scalded his mouth.

"I should go," he said, eyeing the baked goods in the basket. He was hungry. He was always hungry, but suddenly he didn't trust anything he hadn't prepared himself.

"Finn, are you okay?" Christopher was full of concern. "I have fresh coffee brewing. And look...I made your favourite cupcakes. Chocolate sea-salt caramel."

"Yeah. I noticed." He swallowed. Hard.

"This trial's been awfully hard on you," Christopher said, his tone coaxing. "Marcel and I are...worried about you. And of course we can't hide our curiosity. This is the biggest case to hit our people in years!"

"Have a cake." Marcel's gruff tone took on a warmer edge. Finn couldn't resist. His teeth sank into the velvety goodness. The sea-salt crystals offset the sweetness of the caramel. These were Christopher's newest creations for the bakery. He called them breakfast cupcakes because the icing that would normally top the cake was infused inside it in delectable ribbons. Finn's mouth watered from the explosion of fantastic flavours.

"You know, nobody's trying to entrap you or trick you. This is a huge case and I want the gossip. I can't believe how closed-mouthed everyone on the jury is being," Marcel griped. "How am I supposed to feel when our best friend won't even tell us a damned thing?"

"Marcel!" Christopher's voice came out in a shriek.

"I'm scared," Finn said finally when he'd consumed the last crumb. He really was. Not just of Kennedy, but the awfulness that had become his life. He was afraid the trial would never be over. He was afraid that, one by one, all the jurors would meet horrible fates.

"Well, I can understand that," Marcel said finally.

Finn was relieved. "You can?"

"Yes. You don't trust me. If Christopher was here alone, you'd be singing like the proverbial canary."

"Marcel!" Christopher sounded appalled.

"I should go," Finn mumbled. He kept his head down. "Thanks for breakfast."

He shuffled out the door, with Christopher rushing after him.

"Oh, Finn, I'm so sorry," Christopher whispered when they reached the back door. "He's so jealous of our friendship and it's so stupid. Please don't hate him."

"I don't." *I hate him as much as I hate this trial*.

He gave Christopher what he hoped was a reassuring smile then strolled to the beach. He'd take a nice long run and head back home...to bed. He'd watch something light and fun. He liked movies about the ocean. Maybe an oldie but goodie, like *Splash*.

He broke into a comfortable pace, feeling the hard-packed sand under his feet working his leg muscles. In just two months, his rock-solid body had gone a bit soft. He didn't have time for his usual, strenuous workouts and he missed them. The water lapped beside him, the sound of the ocean's rhythm soothing him.

And then...

He heard a roar and the waves swelled up high. He stopped and stared. He'd never seen seven-foot waves this close to the shoreline. A man appeared from the middle of the break, coming towards him.

Finn stopped. He'd never seen anything like him. The almost naked, wild-haired, six-foot tall man came straight at him, closing his hands around Finn's throat. He was shorter than Finn but oh, so much stronger. He dragged him into the ocean, Finn's cries for help gurgling in his throat.

The man dragged him down...down...and Finn realised he was drowning. He fought off his attacker, kneeing him in the groin. The man wore a loin cloth that felt slick and slippery as Finn kicked him again. The grip on his throat loosened. One hand fell away when Finn bit into it. He tasted of brine and endless sea-salt. The stranger roared as Finn rolled, like a whale, getting the man underneath him.

Finn broke the surface, screaming, "Help! Help!"

The man below grabbed him again, looking surprised that Finn was fighting him so hard.

Finn bit the free hand that came at him again and he karate-chopped the other hand struggling for purchase at his throat. He felt the attacker's thumb pressing into his windpipe. He was blacking out when he heard shouting and rapid footfalls, and the next thing he knew, Christopher was in the water with him, dragging him to safety.

They fell onto the sand, Finn coughing and spluttering.

"Oh my God…he was trying to kill me," Finn moaned.

"Who was he?" Christopher gasped. He was on top of Finn and quickly turned him over, pressing on Finn's back. Water and seaweed spewed out of him.

The two men kept coughing and struggling for breath as Marcel ran towards them.

"What the hell's going on?" he demanded.

"This man…he tried to drown Finn. He—" Chris sat up on the sand, looking around, choking on a cough. "Where the hell did he go?"

Finn struggled for composure. His whole body ached. He could barely speak, his voice coming out in a hoarse whisper. He turned around to a sitting position.

"It was the weirdest thing I ever saw. A huge wave came right out of nowhere and this man walked out of it and grabbed me. He dragged me into the water and tried to drown me."

"Really." Marcel looked furious, his arms folded. "And where is this mysterious person now?"

Finn and Christopher gazed out at the tame waves.

"It happened. It was real." Finn's throat felt like it was coated in sand. He turned to Christopher. "You saved my life. Thank you."

"We need to get you inside," Christopher said. "Marcel, help me."

They lifted him to his feet and Marcel's expression changed. They got inside the house.

"Describe this man to me," he said, pacing the kitchen as Christopher gave Finn a towel and a fresh cup of coffee.

Finn did his best even though to his own mind, the whole thing now sounded deranged.

"We have a big problem here." Marcel interrupted Finn's rambling description.

Aw, hell. He doesn't believe me. My God...he came out and found Christopher on top of me...what must he think?

"Marcel, believe me —"

"Oh, I believe you." Marcel looked grim. "I see the bruises on your face and neck now. You do realise he's not going to stop until he kills you too, right?"

Finn's blood froze. His teeth began to chatter. "What do you mean, me too?"

Marcel grimaced. "Like I said, we have a problem." He lifted his hands in a gesture of helpless surrender. "I'm late for work, but I'm sure that under these special circumstances, nobody's going to penalise me. I'm going to call Ephyrus Bainbridge right now."

Finn stared at him. What was Marcel up to, calling Bainbridge?

"He'll disbar me. He'll take away my powers...oh my God. He'll think I told you stuff!"

Marcel scoffed. "Nonsense. Nobody can blame you for being attacked." He held up a finger. "However, for the time being — until we can get you some medical attention and some protection — you're staying here with us."

He picked up his cell phone and began pressing numbers.

Finn panicked. "I can't stay here!"

"You can and you will," Christopher said, putting his arm around Finn's shoulders. "Here, sweetie, drink some of this."

He poured something into Finn's coffee, the smell wafting up to Finn's nose, sending his thoughts to faraway places—images of handsome mermen, ferny dells…a beautiful sunrise…

"Drink, sweetie."

"Hmm?" Finn's mind turned fuzzy. He didn't want to leave the handsome merman. He drank deeply, the merman's face coming into sharper view. Oh, he was handsome.

"That's better." Christopher's voice soothed his soul, but didn't interrupt the dream. He allowed the other man to steer him to the sofa. He sipped some more before Christopher took the cup away from him and urged him to lie down. The magical dream filled Finn's senses—the merman smiling, stroking his face as Christopher's hand touched his cold cheek. He tucked a pillow under Finn's head and a soft blanket around him.

"I think we averted shock," he heard Christopher say, his voice seeming to come from a distant galaxy as the merman crouched beside Finn now, his face full of love.

"Good." Marcel's tone was terse. Finn's eyes drifted shut as he heard the feared jurist say, "I wish I could say it *was* a good morning, Ephyrus. Unfortunately, there's been another attack…"

* * * *

"Mr. Garrison. Mr. Garrison?"

Finn heard the voice calling to him. He didn't want to wake up. Not only did he feel all golden and floaty, but the merman was doing nice things to his cock that no man had done to him in years.

"Mr. Garrison, please."

Finn's eyes opened slowly and he looked up into three faces staring at him. Marcel Paradis, Christopher, and a third man sitting on the sofa beside him. Holy crap, it hadn't been a bad dream. The merman swam away, his gossamer fins receding in Finn's mind. Finn wanted to scream at the unfairness of losing such a fantastic sleep.

"Mr. Garrison, my name is Phillip Sedgwick and I'm an attorney for—"

"I know who you are. You're Daine's boyfriend. He and Christopher run my favourite bakery in the whole world."

Christopher laughed.

Phillip gave him a wonderful smile. "Yes, I'm that, too. But my day job is...well, my *main* work is being an attorney for Arden, Bainbridge, Chinook and Damek."

"Oh." They were back to the frickin' trial again. His spirits sank. The bloody, bloody, *bloody* trial.

"Mr. Garrison—"

"Please call me Finn."

Phillip Sedgwick inclined his head in acknowledgement. "Finn. We don't have much time." He paused, as if trying to choose his words carefully. "The attack on you was the third on a juror for the Camelot trial. You are the only one who has survived."

Finn tried to sit up, but his chest and arms felt like lead.

Marcel and Christopher hurried to help him, propping pillows and cushions behind his back.

Finn coughed. His throat still felt bad.

"You mean…the other jurors…*died*?"

"I'm afraid so."

"But the hit and run victim…they said it was a minor injury. That he just needed a couple of days off."

"He died." Phillip gave him a meaningful look. "As a matter of fact, he drowned."

"Wait a minute…drowned?"

Phillip nodded.

"But…I'm confused. I thought he was in his car?"

"He was. And as far as I know, he's the only person I ever heard of that got hit by a tidal wave in the middle of Union Square."

"Oh my God."

Phillip looked at him. "The first juror drowned in two inches of bathwater. We were able to keep her death a secret but since so many civvies saw the tidal wave yesterday, that's proving harder to keep quiet."

Civvies. It was a fond nickname for humans used by some members of the superpowers fraternity—short for civilians. Some members of the superpowers community used far worse terms. Thanks to the *Harry Potter* franchise, the term 'Muggles' was sometimes used in a derogatory way, but 'civvies' was kind. It also suggested, as Phillip was doing so now, that humans were innocent civilians in a growing war between good and evil being played out in front of them.

"The attack on you was brazen, considering you were in full view of civvies…and Justice Paradis."

Finn's head swivelled up to Marcel.

"So now we're all in danger?" Finn asked, his voice coming out in a hoarse whisper.

"No. Christopher hasn't been able to come up with a description, but you saw the attacker, according to what I've heard. Have you seen him before?"

"Never."

"Would you recognise him again?"

"In a heartbeat."

"That's not good." Phillip looked worried. "Since you've survived, the perpetrator will keep on trying...until he succeeds."

Finn shivered.

He wants me dead...for no reason at all.

Phillip interrupted his thoughts. "We've been working hard to plant a story of a burst water main. The Earth Council has even jumped in to help. As you know, the four branch councils rarely work together, but the Earth Council surprised us by drumming up a sink hole to match the Water Council's burst water main."

"Why is this happening?" Finn asked. "I mean...this was supposed to be a straightforward case."

"You really think so?" Phillip looked incredulous. "Forgive me...but it's been bedlam from day one. We couldn't keep a jury seated because of nebulous threats...strange home floodings, you name it. Now, three jurors have been attacked and you are all the ones who have seen Kennedy. I mean, you have *seen* him, right?"

Finn gulped and nodded. "Oh, yes. I..." he shuddered involuntarily. "Yes, I have."

The three men all looked at him. He could never forget the first moment the sea monster dubbed 'Kennedy' first appeared in the courtroom. It had been a harrowing experience. Composed of water, bearing jagged teeth, numerous heads and stinking of sewage, he'd been a terrible, frightening sight.

"You are aware that the majority of the jurors couldn't see him, right?" Phillip asked.

Finn hesitated. "No, frankly. On the rare occasions we all talked, some people openly admitted to being frustrated that they couldn't see him. A few claimed to see him but I didn't believe them. One of them was that female juror, what was her name? Nancy — "

"Nancy Sugarman," Phillip supplied.

"Right. And now you tell me she drowned. But the other juror...what was his name? Hill Jacobs. He definitely saw him."

"How do you know?"

Finn leaned a little close to Phillip. "I knew he could see him because Kennedy lashed out at him one time in the courtroom and Hill freaked out. Kennedy screamed he wasn't getting a fair trial. He said he was being framed. For some reason, he lashed out at Hill. I've never seen a defendant attack a juror before. I was sitting right next to Hill. He saw one of those big, snake-like arms coming at him and got out of the way just in time."

Phillip looked stunned.

"I hadn't heard about this incident. When did it happen?"

"Two days ago. You know...Kennedy is about the ugliest, most frightening thing I've ever seen."

"How come some jurors can see him and others can't?" Christopher wanted to know. "I've been following the trial and the little that's leaked out indicates only the Mages and Judges can see him."

"I'm a Mage," Finn said. "I know I've never told you that...and in Bermuda, where I live, I'm a practicing psychic."

Christopher smiled at him. "I often wondered about that. You seem so intuitive."

"Did you...were you able to see him right away?" Phillip asked, looking genuinely interested to know.

Finn shrugged. "To be honest, no. It was more of a...feeling. By the end of his first day in the courtroom, I saw him. He was huge. I mean he's like this big, giant, white floating mass of a thing."

"He sounds like a blancmange," Christopher said.

Finn smiled. "Blancmange is a delicious treat. The monster is not."

"Apparently, his father disagrees," Phillip said. "He's doing everything in his power to protect his offspring. Kennedy has appeared to several civvies, resulting in him assaulting two of them. One died, as you know. It is for the court to decide his fate and it is the most unusual case to be tried in the Water Court for two hundred years."

"Well, if his father can't control him," Marcel said, "we have to follow legal procedure."

"Of course." Phillip nodded. "Since Kennedy's own father has been powerless to stop him, we did what we had to do...with terrible consequences."

Finn said nothing. He was aware of Kennedy having a different proper name, but all kinds of taboos surrounded the usage of it.

People in the superpowers and human communities knew of him and legend had it that if you spoke his name aloud, bad things befell you, especially at sea. And now, it seemed, even if you were not. But nobody spoke his name. They called him Kennedy. The sea monster seemed to like it.

Since the trial involved the royal family's youngest son, the case had taken on mythic proportions, conjuring images of Camelot. Then, of course, there was the idea of one of the most prominent American families—the Kennedys. The sea monster being given the name of Kennedy for all intents and purposes went a long way to assuaging his father's fury over the unprecedented trial.

If convicted, however, there would be no fairy tale ending. Only death. The monster would be destroyed. No great loss as far as Finn was concerned.

"The problem is this. You are now the only juror left who is psychic and who can actually see this rotten bastard," Marcel interrupted his thoughts.

"Thanks, Dad." Phillip rolled his eyes. He returned his gaze to Finn. "As my father-in-law put it so well, we need you now, more than ever. The trial won't be able to proceed without you. I can guarantee your protection."

"How?"

"A full time bodyguard. A Water Marshal."

Finn stared at him. "I've done a lot of trials and never heard of that. What is a Water Marshal?"

"He's law enforcement. A cross between a bodyguard and the US Marshal Service. You would be under his care twenty-four-seven. I have somebody in mind I think you'll like. Ty Anglin."

Finn thought for a moment. Phillip had said this as though Finn should recognise the name, but he didn't.

"Did you say Anglin?"

Phillip nodded.

"As in 'angling'? Like fishing?"

"No." Phillip arched a brow. "Like Anglin."

Finn felt his cheeks flush.

"Why do you think I'll like him?" he asked, the words slipping out before he could stop them.

"He's worked on some very interesting mythological capers in your part of the world. He's also not bad looking."

Phillip's grin disarmed Finn and he found himself relaxing.

"Are you up to the challenge?" Phillip asked. "I mean, I will understand if you want to step down from the jury."

"What? And leave myself vulnerable to attack? No." Finn shook his head. "I have nothing to lose. Not really. And I hate bullies."

"Good man," Phillip said and pulled out his cell phone. "I was hoping you'd say that."

"What was in that coffee you gave me?" Finn asked Christopher. "I could sure use some of that right now."

Christopher smiled. "I gave you a pretty good dose, didn't I? Did you see a merman?"

"Oh, yes."

"Well, I'll give you some of the potion to take home with you. For now, I'll give you just one drop, to help you relax. You look much better now."

"Thanks. I feel better."

Finn was disappointed when Christopher squeezed off a single drop into his topped-up coffee. He sniffed and got a hint of the merman…enough to make him smile. Tonight, when he was alone, he'd drink the potion neat, if he had to, and catch up on the naughty things the merman had started with him.

"Hey, Ty," he heard Phillip saying. "Got a case for you."

Finn sipped. And waited.

Chapter Two

Ty Anglin picked up the call a little after nine. He was exhausted after a long night of dealing with the family of the murdered juror in the Camelot trial. Hill Jacobs had been a successful businessman, loving husband and father who had been seated on many juries across the globe. Ty had spent the evening with the man's entire family, now congregated in the fallen juror's Upper Haight home.

Mr. Jacobs' beloved daughter had become traumatised, going into early labour. Ty had taken her to the hospital. Now she was back in her parents' home. A false alarm. This had been a harrowing experience for everyone concerned.

Ty put his key in the car door, glancing up and down the street as he answered his cell phone. He half expected to see a tidal wave heading his way and shook off the thought.

Haight-Ashbury—home of hippies, beatniks, poets, singers, thinkers, 1967's Summer of Love, peace, pot and *hey, man*—had been the beacon of hope for thousands of people for decades. Now its escutcheon had blood all over it. And Ty didn't like it at all.

"Anglin," he answered. He was in a bad mood. It bugged the hell out of him that Hill Jacobs had reluctantly taken the Camelot trial because he was about to become a grandfather for the first time. He'd wanted to be close to his daughter when her due date approached.

And now he was dead and nothing could bring him back.

Ty moved behind the wheel of his red Ferrari wondering how Hill's wife would cope without him. They'd been married for forty-three years and in the few hours since his passing, she'd forgotten three times already that she no longer needed to remind Hill to take his heart pills and his blood pressure medicine. A few times she thought she could hear his voice, then dissolved into tears when she realised she heard the voices of phantom wishes.

This had been an especially tough and harrowing case. First there had been Nancy Sugarman a few weeks ago…now this. When would it end?

Ty tried hard to find the positive in all of this. When he heard Phillip Sedgwick's voice, he smiled. He liked Phillip. He was a hot guy, but unfortunately he was taken. There was something really alluring about him, though. He was whip-smart and kind. Ty tried not to imagine the guy naked and listened intently to the attorney's unbelievable tale.

"And he survived?" he asked, seriously impressed that this Finn Garrison had fought off such a violent attack.

"Yes. And he says he remembers what the attacker looked like. He's willing to continue with the trial."

"Huh." Ty's mood improved. "This guy's got *huevos*."

"He sure does. Listen, Ty, I promised him protection," Phillip said. His voice dropped. "I promised him you'd handle things for him."

"Me?" Ty felt the fury mounting inside him. He was exhausted. He was angry. And they were no closer to nailing the sonofabitch who'd knocked off two jurors. Now he'd tried to get at a third. When would it stop?

"Where is this guy now?" Ty scrawled down the address and blinked. "Wait a moment. Isn't that where Justice Paradis lives?"

"Yes," Phillip said. "My father-in-law. Look, Finn lives two doors down from them. The attack happened right outside their house. Marcel's partner, Christopher Fire, rescued him."

Shit. This mofo is getting more daring. His thoughts raced.

"He can't stay at the Paradis house. Next the murderer will be going after Marcel and his partner."

"Yes, I know." Phillip sounded aggrieved. "Could you come over so we can work all this out? Please?"

"Okay."

Ty ended the call. He was pissed. There went his weekend. All he wanted to do was hole up with some beer and some gay porn. Maybe a funny movie to watch. Did he have any funny gay porn? Well…nothing that was intentionally funny.

He drove across the Golden Gate Bridge heading south to Half Moon Bay. Punching numbers on his cell phone, he talked over his office secretary's customary greeting via his dashboard radio.

"Becca. I need any background info you can get me on Finn Garrison, a juror in the Camelot trial."

"Sure thing, boss. Anything else?"

He traced sarcasm but ignored it.

"Yeah. Fax me all the photos we have on file of Kennedy's known family members and associates."

"Will do."

He cut her off before she could make some lewd joke. She was fond of those. He wasn't. The smell of the ocean cooled his overwrought nerves. He craned his neck to get a closer look at the water beneath the bridge. It sparkled like an aquamarine. He thought about the beaches in Barbados. The water there had been a brilliant, cerulean blue. He heard the whir of his fax machine in back. Pages began popping out. Becca called him a few seconds later.

"Boss?"

"Hit me."

"He's a hot tamale," Becca said.

Ty restrained himself from screaming at her. She was a pain in the ass horn dog, this girl. She saw every man in her vicinity as a potential boyfriend.

"All right, what else?" he asked, watching the civvies around him driving like idiots.

"This is his forty-fifth trial. Highly regarded. Lives in Bermuda."

"Bermuda." Ty leant back in his seat a little. Finn Garrison must have some extraordinary powers to be assigned duty in Bermuda, what with that psychic vortex known as the triangle in the same area.

"He teaches swimming to children and adults. His speciality is water-phobes and people with chronic illnesses. They come from all over the world for the healing powers of Bermuda's waters and for...him. I think that's kinda cool, don't you?"

Ty stopped himself from agreeing aloud. So far this guy sounded special — and to think his life was now in jeopardy.

"Is he a Mage?"

"Yep."

"Married?"

"Nope. Nothing in the report here. He's also done some psychic work, finding lost people, lost ships, that sort of thing."

Intriguing. "Anything else?"

"He's hot."

"Yeah. You mentioned that." Ty ended the call.

She called right back. "There is one other thing."

"What's that?" he barked, hoping to put off any notion she had of making any more personal comments.

"When Hurricane Fabian hit Bermuda in oh-three, he single-handedly saved sixteen people from a sinking ferry. He received a commendation from the city." She fell silent. She was obviously reading a report. "Huh."

"What?" he asked.

"There's never been a trace of the ferry found."

"Oh, that's interesting. Can you fax that report to me?"

"No problem," she said. "There's one other last thing."

"Lemme guess. He's hot?"

"Naw. I already told you that." She paused. He could hear her breathing on the other end of the call, the sound travelling through his on-board speaker system.

"What?" he snapped.

"He was born on a shipwrecked boat off the Florida coast. He ended up moving to Bermuda with his family when he was a kid. He's a bit of a local celebrity. He's found more remains of shipwrecks than anyone else. And, get this. He's found actual treasure from a couple of Spanish galleons and turned them all over, unlike some people, free of charge to the Bermuda government, on condition of the items remaining on the island and never to be sold or lent to other museums."

Something itched at the back of Ty's mind. The memory of another 'explorer' who received a fortune from the Bermuda government for lost treasures discovered on the bottom of the ocean floor.

He began to wonder what Finn Garrison looked like. He let Becca babble. Another document popped out of his fax machine. He didn't know what he'd expected, but it sure wasn't a skinny runt of a guy with spiky blond hair. And…Jesus God, he had so many pimples his face looked like a relief map of Switzerland.

"This is him?" he gaped at the image as he kept one eye on the freeway and groped in the back seat for the documents that kept arriving. *This was the guy she thought was so hot?*

"I haven't sent you his picture," she purred. "You want to see him?"

Fuck, yes. "Of course. I want to know who I'm looking for, Becca."

"No problem."

Another page spat out of the fax machine. He snatched it up and grinned. He felt a definite tightness in his pants as he gazed at the manly man staring back at him. In the old days, they would have called Finn Garrison a he-man. He looked like one of the 'after' shots of a skinny dude all muscled up following a serious workout regime. Thick, dark hair, big, expressive brown eyes and a killer body. The photo was taken of him on a beach. Ty missed the turn off for the short freeway that would take him to Half Moon Bay and cursed himself.

As he hit a set of traffic lights, he quickly read the note under the photo—*Finn Garrison rescues and rehabilitates local wildlife in his spare time.*

Ty's grin turned wider. *Of course he does.*

"Told you," Becca trilled. "He's yummy."

Ty felt indignation swelling in his belly. "We have a job to do protecting this man, Becca. By the way, who's the crazy blond guy you sent me the picture of?"

The lights turned green and he moved forwards, picking up the trail again for the Pacific Coast Highway.

"Crazy? Are you kidding? That's my new boyfriend."

Aw, geez…no accounting for taste.

"And you sent it to me because…?"

"Just letting you know some men find me irresistible."

Aw, crap. "Okay, kid, gotta go."

He ended the call and kicked in his onboard navigation system, which guided him as he wended his way past a main street that looked filled with charming stores and cafes. He finally arrived at the Paradis house on North Cabrillo Highway. He parked in the driveway behind an SUV, grabbed his work satchel and stuffed all the pages Becca had faxed into it.

Though the address was officially a highway, it was a rustic one, with plenty of trees, singing birds—the whole nine sunshiny, beachy yards. All the homes faced the ocean. He knocked on the door. An older man, good looking and just getting grey at the temples, greeted him.

"Marshal Anglin?"

"Yes."

"Marcel Paradis."

Ty shook his hand and felt a surge of heat shoot right up his fingers. *The old show off.* He worked to hide the grimace of pain he felt and stepped inside the house.

Mesmerised by its clean lines and simple beauty, he was even more dazzled by a gorgeous blond man who stepped up to him. "I'm Christopher Fire. So glad you could be here."

Sheesh. How did that old fart get such a hot guy?

Ty felt a tug of protectiveness when Finn Garrison came over to him. The man looked exhausted, and— Ty was shocked to see—Finn's face, neck and torso were covered in livid bruises.

"We need photographs of your injuries," he said in lieu of a greeting. He needed to focus on Finn, not let his own attraction get in the way.

The word *hello* seemed to die on Finn's lips.

"I'm Ty Anglin," he said gruffly, reaching for his cell phone. He was alarmed at the extensive injuries the other man had received. He even had flecks of blood in his eyes, an indication of near-death by strangulation. How the heck had he survived such a savage assault?

"May I call you Ty?" Finn asked.

"You may call me Tyros," he said. Again he saw enthusiasm wane from Finn Garrison's face. *Oh, man.* This wasn't the way he wanted things to go. He sounded like a total bastard. Why was he letting this situation get to him? Or was it Marcel and Christopher's presence with their undeniable Fire-Power? "Sorry, Ty is fine."

Finn seemed to relax a little, but he still looked a little wary as they went into the large kitchen.

"Coffee?" Christopher asked.

"Hmm? Oh, sure."

"We took photos already. If you give me your email address, I'll send them to you," Phillip Sedgwick said, clapping Ty on the shoulder.

"Oh, thanks." Ty felt totally befuddled. He'd had no sleep and now he was going to have to protect a man who was bigger and stronger than he was.

What if I fail?

He took the proffered cup of coffee. For some reason, being in the Fire Judge's house made him lose focus.

Bet he's a tiger in the sack. Oh, boy. I can feel it now. He and Christopher are wild for each other. He remembered suddenly that the jurist had left the court system for several years until a spectacular Fire Trial against his son, Daine. He and Christopher had come back to town for it. Now, he was back and his power was undeniable.

I think I'm getting a fever.

"Milk? Sugar?" Christopher settled him down, soothing his jangled psyche with specifics. Ty sat at the breakfast bar beside Finn, the others standing around him. He sipped his coffee, his brain coming into focus.

"Sorry. Had a rough night."

Finn nodded as if he understood.

"I worked on the tidal wave case. I suppose you've all heard about that."

"Yes, we have." Marcel Paradis propped a stool opposite him. "What's the game plan for our friend Finn?"

Oh, boy. I can't screw up. He's his friend.

"Cupcake?" Christopher asked.

"Huh? Oh, yeah, thanks." Ty bit into it, wondering why he felt so helpless and confused.

I gotta get out of this house. The old man...well, he's not so old...maybe fifty, but he's exerting his strength. Heck...am I breaking out in a sweat?

His thoughts stopped spiralling as he ate his cake and drank his coffee. He felt normal again. How...why...he didn't know, but his head cleared and the fever vanished.

"We need to get Finn to a safe house," Ty said, pleased that he was able to speak and sound like himself again.

"You mean I can't stay here at the beach?" Finn asked, looking crestfallen.

"Heck, no. Christopher, you got another cupcake, please?"

Christopher handed him another one and topped off his coffee.

"No, I'm afraid not. We can still run on the beach, but not this one. There are a few of them up here, but we have to break up your routine. For now, it's safest if you come and stay with me."

"Where do you live?"

"Redwood City."

"Where's that?" Finn asked.

"Twenty-five minutes from here. It's farther inland, but a very nice place. Inland is very good, Finn. I saw first-hand what happened to the other juror, Hill Jacobs. I don't think this perpetrator will travel all the way to Redwood City. At least, I hope not."

He drained his coffee. "Speaking of which, do you recognise any of these men?" He pulled out his gallery of photos. Finn looked through them all, taking his time.

"No," he said, shaking his head. "Who's the weird blond dude?"

"Nobody." He waved his hand as if shooing away a fly. "My assistant threw that one in."

"So, what do we do next?" Finn looked miserable.

"We go to your house and pack your gear then I want to take you to see the Mage of Flowers. I've been trying to reach her but she never picks up her phone."

"I know where she is," Christopher piped up. "She's at the bakery. She's done wonders helping us create a new line of edible flowers for our cupcakes. She'll be there for the next couple of hours. Want me to ask her to stay for a while?"

"Yes. Please tell her we're on our way."

Ty hoisted himself to his feet. "Let's get you packed up, guy."

* * * *

Fabulous Cupcakes, in the heart of San Francisco's college district, had lines going around the corner. Both Finn and Ty were shocked.

"Dang, they must be some great cupcakes," Ty remarked.

"Well, I'm sure the cakes are a draw, but I've heard the bakery's become a kind of hub for all the elemental superpowers. They've turned it into a neutral ground to meet, exchange ideas…recipes even."

"No kidding." Ty seemed surprised. "I bet that's Christopher's influence."

Finn smiled, his gaze falling away from Ty's face. Ty had been trying to decide if Finn was gay or straight. As he'd walked through the man's house collecting his belongings, he couldn't tell…although he thought some of the DVDs lined up for his viewing screamed *gay*.

Now everything was packed and inside Ty's trunk, and Ty was certain the man was gay. *And* that he had a crush on Christopher. Interesting…

They parked across the road in the college campus parking lot as Phillip had instructed them. Finn tugged at the long-sleeved shirt he'd donned in spite of the warm weather. He had it buttoned almost to his throat and down to his wrists. He touched his throat now, then adjusted his sunglasses.

"You look fine," Ty assured him.

They crossed over to the entrance of Fabulous Cupcakes, where the scent of key lime cupcakes — the flavour of the day — wafted out, making Ty's mouth water.

"I'm still hungry," Finn said, looking surprised.

They excused themselves as they moved past people lined up out front. Some people grudgingly allowed them passage, others tried to block them.

"Wait your turn," they groused.

"Easy, easy, we're not going to buy anything," Ty assured them. With the powers vested in him, he could squeeze a man's hand and give him anything from a sneezing fit to double pneumonia. It came in handy with pesky civvies.

Inside the bakery, a young woman stood side by side with Daine Paradis and Christopher — selecting, placing and packaging incredible-looking morsels. Even Phillip Sedgwick had been galvanised into duty on the register.

The young woman looked up.

"There's a line," she said, looking harried.

"Lilly, this is Water Marshal Anglin," Christopher interjected. "He's here to see Easter Sunrise."

"Oh. Sorry." Lilly looked flustered.

"Could you take our two guests upstairs, please?"

"But—"

"Please," Christopher repeated. She nodded and beckoned Finn and Ty towards the back. They passed by the kitchen which looked like a well-run but crazed factory. Ty and Finn both stopped to look through the wide-open doors at the trays of cakes being lifted from multi-stacked ovens, others being iced by a crew of men of varying ethnicities. None of them looked up, each too busy with his duties.

Although it looked chaotic, the kitchen was clean and the speed and efficiency of production looked...exemplary.

"It's bedlam, I know," Lilly sighed. "I came here to work part-time and now I'm Daine's full-time assistant. Ever since Cairo left—she's Christopher's sister, you know—and she started her own business...not that she was such a huge help here, you know..."

She prattled on as she led the way, turning around to talk to them.

"Now that Christopher is taking over a new space next door for pizza and pasta, it will be a lot more work and a lot more madness. Not that I mind. I love the work and I love that he teaches me. Correction. He doesn't teach me. I steal my lessons. I watch and I observe."

She led Ty and Finn to a set of stairs that led to an upper floor. Ty felt the mingling of elements. Finn must have felt it too. One second, he felt heat...the next—air, water and earth. They swelled and rose as they ascended the steps, enveloping him like an invisible cloud.

Lilly thrust open the door and around twenty people inside what looked like an upstairs apartment stopped speaking.

"They're here for Easter," Lilly announced. She turned to leave, dropped her gaze to Ty's footwear and leaned into him.

"Cowboy boots. You know what they say about men in cowboy boots."

"No," he said, startled. "What do they say?"

"Ggrrrrrrf!" She growled in his ear then took the steps down two at a time.

"I think she just undressed you with her voice," Finn said, a big grin on his face.

Ty glanced at him. The guy wasn't kidding. Why couldn't guys make passes at him this way? Why was it always women? And what was with Lilly and footwear, anyway?

"Come on in," a woman said, ushering them to the kitchen. Here, too, food seemed to be in various stages of production but the atmosphere was calmer, quieter.

"Well, as I live and breathe…Tyros Anglin."

"Easter!" he was genuinely pleased to see his cousin again. It had been some years but she was a fantastic healer and he trusted her implicitly.

Finn stared at the five-foot woman with the green, purple and gold hair and clothing. She was one of the superpowers' secret weapons—a healer of the first order. She'd come out of a long retirement to help the superpowers world in a few recent cases and had connected with Christopher and Daine in a profound way, according to what Chris had told Ty. Now he hoped she would use her healing powers to help Finn.

"Magenta," she said to the woman beside her, "can we have a few minutes of privacy, please?"

The woman piping ruby-coloured frosting onto pale, cream-coloured cakes didn't look pleased but left the kitchen, closing the door to the rest of the apartment.

"Right, let's have a look at you." Her gaze remained on Finn who slowly took off his sunglasses. She tsked somewhere deep in her throat.

"And the shirt too, please," she whispered.

Finn did as he was told, looking embarrassed.

She pointed to two seats against the wall.

"Tyros, bring those to the table, please."

He did. Easter told them both to sit, then took her own chair, sitting knee-to-knee with Finn, studying his face, neck and hands.

"Webbed hands did this. I see no evidence of poisoning." She held Finn's hands in hers.

"Tyros, I'll need Magenta's help. I don't want to let go of Finn yet, okay?"

"Okay." He was reluctant and knew it showed.

"She's a first class horticulturalist. She knows more about the healing powers of plants than even I do. Christopher did good suppression work on Finn. It's a start. But I want to lift the shock from his system with as little trauma to his psyche as possible."

Ty didn't have to be persuaded. He agreed immediately.

"Magenta." Easter spoke softly, but the woman must have been strongly in tune with Easter, because she returned to the kitchen immediately, closing the door behind her. She did a double-take when she saw Finn's condition.

"Let's start with wild rose," Easter said. She kept holding Finn's hands, staring into his face.

Ty watched Magenta pull out two tiny pale rose-coloured cakes, saw her pipe a little frosting and top them off with rose petals.

"I'm going to release one of your hands," Easter said to Finn who nodded. "I want you to eat the first cake, chewing it fast, the second a little slower. We always serve two cakes. The first to taste, the second to savour."

Finn followed her instructions and moaned around the obviously wonderful flavours in his mouth.

"I gave you rose to dispel the helplessness you feel," Easter said. "You feel your best wasn't good enough, but it was. Look at you—you survived." She looked very emotional. "I am very sorry for what happened to you, Finn."

She waited until he ate the second cake.

"Rose and sage for the next one," Easter said. To Finn she reported, "Sage will help your psyche forget the damage done. Then we can work on curing your physical ailments."

"You can do that?"

Easter smiled. "I can do that."

She coaxed him through tiny cakes topped with Johnny jump-ups, violets, bee balm and calendula. Ty was transfixed.

"Squash blossom for you," she told Ty who happily consumed two cakes that made him feel refreshed and better than a full eight hours of sleep could have done.

"I'm sending you home with rose and lavender cakes. A dozen each for the weekend. On Monday morning, before the trial resumes, please stop by so I can check that the flowers are holding up," Easter said, her small hands running along Finn's now unblemished face and throat. "How do you feel?"

Finn shook his head. "I can't believe it. I feel really good."

"Excellent. Ty, take good care of our friend."

"I'd like to hug you if I may," Finn said.

Easter jumped to her feet and held out her arms. They held each other long and hard. When she finally pushed Finn away, there were tears in both their eyes.

"The little boy you tried to save from drowning a long time ago…" She shook her head. "He has become one of your guides. He helped you fight off the beast. He wants you to know he is always with you, but he wants to you to stop grieving him. Okay?"

Tears flowed down Finn's face.

"Oh, my God…you know about him?"

"Oh, yes. He was the first one here. He's…" She looked around. "He comes and goes. He's in a place of great healing. He loves you for trying to save him."

Ty was speechless when Finn turned to him, his face free of the awful bruises, his beautiful, expressive eyes no longer flecked with blood.

"You look great," he said.

Finn gave him a radiant smile. "Thanks, so do you."

They took their packages of cupcakes and went downstairs to say goodbye to Christopher and Phillip.

"Wow, you look great." Christopher beamed at Finn. "Here's a carry bag. Don't forget to put the drops I gave you into some tea or coffee tonight."

Finn laughed. "Don't worry, I won't."

"Here's a small sample of blancmange we're going to start selling when we expand."

"Oh, no," Finn said. "I can't look at that stuff. It reminds me of…you know." His voice dropped. "Kennedy."

"Oh, shoot, I forgot." Christopher grimaced. "Sorry. Well, let me know when you're ready because Easter infused all kinds of good things into this."

* * * *

Finn slept most of the way down to Redwood City. When they approached the city limits of the 101 Freeway, Ty had to stop for gas and groceries. He hated to awaken the guy but even though he'd pumped gas and was able to keep his eye on Finn the whole time, he worried about leaving him alone while he picked up basic foodstuffs. They couldn't just eat cupcakes all weekend.

He needn't have worried. Finn stirred as they pulled into the parking lot of Chavez Supermarket and Taqueria on Arguello Street, around the corner from Ty's house.

"I smell tacos," he said, a sleepy grin on his face.

"That's because we're right outside the best *taqueria* in town."

They got out of the car, walked inside the market and went hog wild buying tea, coffee, a twelve-pack of beer, sandwich makings, a couple of steaks, salad, a barbecued chicken and at Ty's suggestion, the house speciality of steak burritos. They bought them with all the trimmings — guacamole, salsa, sour cream and chips — then hauled the stuff home.

"This place is like Mayberry," Finn enthused.

"It really is. There are so many wonderful little historic sites. Even the fire station has character and a whale of a tale behind it."

"You grew up here?" Finn asked.

"Yep. And it's still my refuge."

As they rolled into Ty's Oak Avenue driveway, Finn sat at attention.

"This is awesome," he breathed. "Wow."

"Thanks." Ty appreciated the compliment. He'd hand-built the place out of actual redwoods and stone ferried in from New England.

They unloaded the car, taking everything inside.

Ty led his guest to the spare room he used both for company and for storage. It was, thank goodness, mercifully free of storage boxes right now, but once his brother and sister-in-law, who lived in nearby Foster City, started Christmas shopping for their kids again, this room would look like holiday central. The idea of Finn not being in the room discomfited him.

"Make yourself at home. You have your own bathroom. I'll get you some fresh bed linens and towels."

"Thank you, this is really kind of you."

"No problem." Ty borrowed a phrase right out of his assistant, Becca's mouth. Finn got his stuff squared away fast and came into the kitchen just as Ty was transferring their Mexican food onto plates. He snapped the tops off two bottles of beer and they ate at the dining room table.

Ty found Finn exceptionally easy to talk to. They chatted about their lives and Bermuda—for which Ty felt a huge affinity. When they'd finished eating, he offered his guest some coffee.

"I'd love that. Wanna watch a movie?" Finn asked.

They even settled amicably on their choice, one of the Matt Damon *Bourne* movies. As the sun set and they sat in front of the TV in the living room, Finn poured some of the contents of a vial into his cup.

"I'm willing to share this," he said. "It's really wonderful."

"What does it do?"

"Gives you a nice, warm, sexy experience. And Christopher has tailored it so that you have a personalised erotic dream."

"No kidding?" Ty thrust his own cup at Finn, who laughed, emptying the rest of the vial into Ty's cup.

"Cheers," Ty said, touched that Finn would share his magical elixir this way. Ty wondered what his dream would be like and hoped it would involve rolling around naked in bed with Phillip.

He sipped his coffee. He didn't have to wait long. He started to feel all good and warm, his mind no longer on the movie. He had a much more exciting one unspooling in his mind.

A naked man lay face down on a wide bed, gyrating on white tousled sheets, the sounds of cawing gulls and the ocean's smooth roar coming in through an open window. Ty stood at the foot of the bed, admiring the perfect, naked ass moving in front of him. The ass seemed very familiar, but he couldn't quite place it. Sensuous and slow though the movements were, they still had him hard and wanting more within seconds. There was something very sexy about the man almost making love to the bed.

Naked himself, Ty moaned at the erotic image and reached forwards to stroke the perfect buttocks in front of him. The taut, soft skin under his fingertips begged for more intimate contact. His hard cock jutted in front of him. He climbed behind the man, kneeling between his legs.

The man sighed, parting his thighs and lifting his ass as if for better access. Ty let his cock run up and down the sweet ass crack in front of him. The man on the bed moaned in anticipation.

"Oh, yeah," he said.

Ty bent down to replace his cock with his tongue, licking the man's ass cheeks. The ass met his tongue thrusts and Ty explored deeper, delving into the crack, reaching under the man's hips to touch his cock. It was rigid. He had to taste it.

"Turn over," he urged and the man did.

He was surprised to see not Phillip, but Finn Garrison lying underneath him, a pleading look in his eyes.

It matched the look Ty felt radiating from his own being. He bent and licked the head of the juicy cock in his firm grip. Dream-Finn moaned, gripping the sheets as if to try to hold on.

Ty licked and teased, tasted and taunted, urging Finn to swift release in his mouth. He was surprised how hard Finn came.

Ty was even more surprised that he could taste roses and cake in the dream-man's sweet liquid. Or was he a dream-man at all?

Chapter Three

Finn had never had such an incredible weekend. At least, not for a long, long time. He didn't want it to end. He'd felt protected and safe and really enjoyed Ty's company. He found himself hopelessly attracted to the man but couldn't tell if Ty liked him. Sometimes he seemed to, sometimes he pulled back.

As for the erotic dreams? They'd kept coming despite the fact that he'd used up all of Christopher's elixir on the first evening. Those moments on the white sheets had been all kinds of magical and he'd never come so hard. He only wished they'd been real. Ty was one hell of an attractive guy with his light brown hair and hazel eyes. And in the dream world he'd been very clearly attracted to him.

But now it was Monday morning and time to return to reality. He had a job to do, much as he hated the thought of it.

They drove across the Golden Gate Bridge back into town bright and early. He'd enjoyed their quiet, private weekend of walking, talking, eating and watching movies, so now the jarring traffic sounds threw him a little. He wished he was back in Ty's house. There were no monsters there.

Ty took him to Fabulous Cupcakes, where a crowd was already forming out front before the place even opened.

"Cairo's Cakes isn't even in the same league by the looks of things," Ty said, as if reading Finn's thoughts.

Indeed, the place across the street looked deserted. What had possessed her to open a rival shop in such close proximity anyway? He shook his head. Surely common sense would have told her to go looking for her own turf.

Daine let them into the bakery, to the chagrin of people waiting out front.

"Just give me two minutes," Daine good-naturedly told his patrons then ushered Ty and Finn into the big bakery kitchen where Easter was putting the finishing touches to some incredible-looking cupcakes.

"Hey, you two," she said. "Say, you're looking much better."

She handed Finn two lavender cakes. "They'll keep you calm today."

When she handed Ty two violet-topped cakes, he quirked a brow at her.

"These will keep you sharp and focused."

Their cakes were soon gone and after a quick thank you to everybody, they waved to Phillip, who sat at a table eating a gigantic cupcake covered in chocolate.

"I'm trying to ignore the death ray stares from the people out front," he said, his head tilting at the collection of faces pressed up at the window. "Just so you know, Bainbridge knows all about what happened to Finn. The bailiffs at the court and the judge have all been informed. There will be no special announcement that Finn will be on the jury today. Everyone is going to act like business as usual."

He licked some chocolate from his fingers. "We managed to keep the attack from being made public. By the way, Finn, you look great."

Finn nodded. "I feel great, thanks to Ty."

Ty seemed pleased at the compliment.

"We should go," he said. "Don't want to be late."

Finn and Ty left the bakery as the doors opened and customers stampeded to the counter.

Finn felt a moment of panic.

"It's okay. I will be in the courtroom right where you can see me at all times," Ty said, his tone reassuring.

They drove down towards the Golden Gate Bridge, but took a turnoff before they reached it. They arrived at a small gate unseen by human eyes and pulled into the parking lot for the Water Court. Being a juror, Finn was given special parking privileges. Ty parked near the above-ground entrance to the grotto that contained the Water Court's judicial rooms.

Inside, they passed security clearance, Ty standing very close to Finn. They descended the wide marble stairs and entered the courtroom in which the jurors were starting to assemble. Finn loved the large room, which looked like it was underwater.

It was.

All four walls were made of glass and caused the place to look like an aquarium. All kinds of sea life swam past — stingrays, sea lions, schools of fish, sea turtles, dolphins, sharks and a whale or two.

The floor consisted of the softest, whitest sand imaginable. There was even the occasional wave that passed over it, leaving rippled traces in the soft surface. Finn's feet had been wet a few times before he'd developed the knack of pulling them up just before the next one hit.

Finn took his seat in the jury box. It was shaped like a giant sea shell, but was padded for comfort. He noticed that Hill Jacobs' seat remained unoccupied. It made him nervous. How were they going to continue the trial with a missing jury member? Or had they managed to replace Hill over the weekend?

He had no idea why, but he looked across to where Ty stood. Ty nodded in a reassuring way...but Finn was a Water Mage. His intuition was strong. Something was about to happen.

Judge Fathom hadn't even taken his seat when a new juror sat beside Finn. One look and he was so shocked he jumped from his seat, stricken. *What the hell?* He glanced back over at Ty.

Ty stared back at him.

"Mister Garrison, please take your seat," the judge said, his voice angry in spite of the sea song lilt to it.

"I can't, Your Honour."

Finn was in a state of full-blown panic now. He had to get away before it was too late. He tried climbing out of the jury box.

"Ty," he screamed when the man beside him grabbed him. He saw Ty running towards him, batting people out of the way.

"It's him! It's him!" Finn shouted.

"Mr. Garrison!" the judge roared.

"Your Honour," Finn yelled as the man's hands reached for his throat. "This is the man who tried to kill me two days ago."

"What?" The judge looked surprised for a moment then shook his head. "That isn't possible. I'm sure you're imagining things. Now, please sit down or I'll have to find you in contempt of court."

Possible or not, the man now had his cold, clammy hands around Finn's throat from behind and was starting to cut off his air supply. Again. The threat of being found in contempt of court was minor compared to the possibility of losing his life. Didn't the judge see what was going on?

Finn fought back with everything he had, but trying to dislodge the murderer's hands proved impossible. His skin was covered in a slithering, slimy layer of—something—making it difficult to get a grip on the bastard. Adding the lack of air and how dizzy he already was, meant he was quickly approaching desperate.

Where the hell was Ty?

A loud roar made its way through the whooshing noise his ears were producing as his air remained cut off. He tried kicking the bastard, but he was in the wrong position to do any damage. The slimy assassin had stayed well outside the reach of his knees this time.

Finally, Ty's welcome face appeared through the fog in front of his eyes. Better yet, the death grip on his throat lightened up as Ty began to claw the man's fingers away one by one.

"Come on, Finn, help me out here." Ty's voice was rough, his breath came in gasps. "Try to hold onto his arms or something so I can see where he is."

What? See where he is? This wasn't making any sense. First the judge, now Ty? At least Ty had believed him, but the situation was going from creepy to scary faster than he would have thought possible.

The struggle seemed to take hours but it couldn't have been more than a few minutes. Finn was exhausted. He slipped in and out of consciousness, then little gusts of air made it through, thanks to Ty's efforts. The moments of reprieve were not enough for the fog in his brain to clear up. But Finn held on, encouraged by the fact that Ty seemed to make progress.

"Yeah, that's it. Keep your hands where they are." Ty sounded out of breath and not from running across the courtroom. "Bastard keeps slipping away."

"Sand," Finn croaked. Shit, his vocal cords were damaged.

"Sand?" Ty frowned then his eyes lit up. "Of course! Someone get me some sand right now."

One of the bailiffs bent down and started hurling handfuls of the stuff from the ground. The next thing Finn knew, the additional friction of small grains of dirt rubbed against his throat.

"Ouch."

"Won't be long," Ty panted.

Ty's grasp on the attacker's slippery fingers must have improved because Finn was finally getting some air. Ty moved around him with the speed of a sailfish on the hunt for prey. Finn collapsed into his seat, grabbing his throat in a futile effort to make the pain go away.

By the time he'd gulped some air into his lungs and was ready to check on Ty's progress, his Water Marshal had not only subdued the attacker but had somehow succeeded in making him visible as well. The entire courtroom was staring at the wild haired man who was lying on the floor on his stomach, his hands pulled behind his back and securely cuffed.

"How?" Finn glanced at Ty.

"Our handcuffs zero-out other superpowers." Ty grinned as he bent down to pull the assassin up.

"Someone made him invisible?" That explained a lot. "I didn't even know that was possible."

"When you're ready, gentlemen." Judge Fathom's voice boomed across the room.

Finn looked up. The judge was red in the face, whether from embarrassment or anger wasn't clear.

"I would like to proceed with this case, but it seems that an interruption is unavoidable." The judge stared at the other jurors as if it was their fault. Maybe he was trying to decide if there were more assassins amongst them. "I will adjourn this case until tomorrow morning. We need to find out what is going on and who has dared interfere in my trial. Whoever is behind this has messed with one juror too many. Not to mention that they have dared send an assassin into a court of law."

Finn changed his judgement to anger. The judge was clearly pissed off.

"Bailiffs, please clear the courtroom." The judge pointed at him, Ty and the glowering attacker. "Messrs Garrison and Anglin, as well as the assassin, will stay."

The bailiffs nodded and started their work, only to be interrupted by a loud roar from the direction of the defendant. Kennedy was trying to resist being led away, but the superpowers' resistant restraints left him no choice. His defence lawyer, a Mr. Brian Pontus, was trying to calm him down, without much luck. Robert Hydros, the Water lawyer working closely with Ephyrus Bainbridge, had a very smug smile on his face.

What the hell was that all about?

The judge turned to him, his eyes changing from a stormy dark grey with hints of lightning to a more mellow deep blue. "Mr. Garrison, do you require medical attention?"

He just needed to be left alone and to have his old life back, thank you very much. But he knew that he wasn't going to get it, at least not in the foreseeable future, so he sighed and shook his head. "I think I'll be okay. But I'd like to get some water, if I may?"

"You will not leave this courtroom." The judge pointed at one of the extra bailiffs who had entered to help their colleagues move the most resistant members of the audience outside. "Get this man some water, Leith."

The burly bailiff nodded and hurried back outside, only to return moments later with a handful of water bottles. He placed them on the seat next to Finn and backed away as if afraid to stick around. Finn shrugged. The first mouthful of water to hit his throat felt like heaven. He gulped more of the cool liquid and felt better. What he wouldn't have given for one of Easter's healing cupcakes right about now.

"Are you really okay?" Ty's eyes carried a reassuring level of worry. "That guy was pretty strong."

"I'll be fine, don't worry. Being a Water Mage, all I really need is some water and some time to heal." Finn smiled and wanted to hug the man.

"If you're sure?" Ty sat down right next to him, close enough to touch. His other hand rested firmly on the scowling attacker, who'd been made to sit down on his other side. "We can insist on following proper procedure, which would be to get Mr. Stranglehold here taken into superpowers police custody straightaway."

"No, I'd rather see if the judge can get something out of this guy first. He does have the right to try, since the incident happened in his courtroom." Finn loved that water law was so—fluid.

"If you're quite ready, gentlemen?" Judge Fathom had an amused smile on his face and was leaning back in his chair as he watched them.

"Sure, we're ready." Ty nodded, but his slight irreverence hadn't gone unnoticed.

"Will you tell us your name?" The judge stared at the would-be murderer, clearly trying to make him speak.

"Wiley Tritos." The man looked straight ahead, stubbornly refusing to make eye contact.

"Who sent you here?" Judge Fathom leant forwards.

"You should know better than to ask. That is something I don't have to tell you." The man laughed.

"What? He has to tell him his name but nothing else?" Finn thought he might have ended up in an old spy movie.

"Technically, the only things he has to tell the court are his name and his house affiliation." Ty tilted his head. "If he's clever, and expects leniency once he gets to his own trial, he will volunteer more information. On the other hand, depending on who sent him, he may be more afraid of the repercussions from their side than the legal aspect of his situation."

"Let's start at the beginning then." The judge frowned at them, but turned back to the scowling prisoner. "Are you associated with the elemental powers of water?"

Wiley nodded.

"Which house?"

Wiley shrank back a little.

"I asked you a question you have no choice but to answer." Judge Fathom put his hands on his table, gripping the edge for support. The leashed fury in his body language made Finn shudder.

Wiley's entire body started shaking.

"Your last name being Tritos, I assume you are associated with the element of water?" The judge narrowed his eyes.

Wiley nodded, his eyes wary.

"Salt water, to be exact?" The judge continued to watch the prisoner very intently.

Wiley nodded again, his tension lifting slightly.

"That makes sense." The judge leant back in his chair looking smug.

The relief pouring off the handcuffed man was almost palpable.

Odd. And way too easy. There was something not quite right here. That silent agreement after all the hesitation was very suspicious. Didn't the judge see what was going on? Finn opened his mouth to speak up, when Ty's hand squeezing his thigh stopped him. He glanced over and saw a minuscule shake of his head.

Oookay.

"Mr. Kennedy obviously has powerful friends." The Judge was furiously writing, filling one sheet after another as he spoke. "I will not venture into speculation about who is behind this assassination attempt, or rather potentially several attempts, but it is rather obvious that the royal house of Neptune stands to benefit if this trial doesn't take place. I will order an investigation of Mr. Kennedy's closest relatives to find out which of them has hired this assassin. I will not have my jurors threatened, or my trial interfered with, any longer."

The judge looked up.

Nobody disagreed.

"That will be all for today, gentlemen." The judge sealed several envelopes and rang the gong which would bring a bailiff back into the room. "I will expect you both back here tomorrow morning, by which time I will make a decision about the continuation of this trial versus a break to allow the legal powers to catch up. Mr. Anglin, I expect you to deliver the prisoner into safe keeping."

Ty nodded briefly. His lips were pressed into a thin line and the hand on Finn's thigh was balled into a fist. The Water Marshal was very angry and trying very hard not to show it.

What the hell was going on?

* * * *

Ty had rarely been this angry. Judge Fathom may have been an excellent jurist, but his abilities as an investigator left a lot to be desired. He shouldn't even have attempted to get the truth out of that murderous bastard. That was the job of law enforcement, and since he needed to stick with Finn twenty-four-seven, there were certain parts of the investigation he'd need help with. Besides, it was always seen as better for the Marshal in charge to be working with local law enforcement.

He needed competent help who wouldn't, and couldn't, be deterred by power games between members of the royal Water House — or worse.

He knew just the detective whom he wanted in charge.

Julian Narragan, originally from Fall River, Massachusetts, was an old college friend and powerful Water Detective. He'd left the Narragansett Bay area only a few months earlier and was quickly establishing himself within the superpowers branch of the SFPD. On top of which — his family allegiance being to estuaries — meant he was guaranteed to be neutral if there really was some sort of salt water versus fresh water issue behind the assassination attempts. Ty was going to call in every single favour owed him to get Julian assigned to this case.

He would get onto that as soon as they left the Water Court building. If only the judge would let them go already.

One of the bailiffs entered and took most of the envelopes from the judge's desk for delivery. He left as quickly as possible, without a backwards glance. Ty wished he could go with him.

"Are you still here?" The judge looked confused, clearly more intent on getting the rest of his paperwork done than on sending them on their way.

"You haven't officially dismissed us." Much as he hated to sit here and wait like an idiot, he wasn't going to annoy a powerful Water Judge by disobeying the rules. Not if he could possibly avoid it.

"Oh, quite." The judge waved a hand at them dismissively as his gaze returned to the surface of his desk. "You can go. I will see you tomorrow morning."

Gritting his teeth, Ty got up, pulling the slightly resistant Wiley with him.

"Come on, let's deliver him to the superpowers prison, then we need to talk to an old friend of mine to make sure this investigation continues full speed...while I make sure you stay alive." Ty winked at Finn to make sure the man knew he was joking...well, sort of.

"You think they're going to try again?" Finn followed him outside and up the marble staircase.

Wiley coughed. Had that been a laugh? Ty wished he could beat him up—just a little—to get some real information out of him. Something more than meets the eye was definitely going on here.

"I don't know. Obviously, I hope not, but I'm not holding my breath."

"Shit." Finn sounded exhausted and fed up.

Ty turned around to look at the other man. His beautiful white skin was bruised around the neck — again — and his eyes had dark shadows around them. He needed some TLC, and soon.

He turned back to focusing on the task at hand, getting the prisoner seated in — more like scrunched into the back of — his Ferrari. Ty then secured him to the door handle with a second pair of handcuffs he always kept handy in the trunk. First things first.

But as he started driving towards the superpowers police station, the thought of someone having tried to kill this wonderful man, twice, got to him. It had probably been the idiot in handcuffs grumbling in the back, but that remained to be proven. He or someone else had already murdered two jurors. There were rumours that Kennedy's father wasn't happy that his youngest son had been put on trial. The most obvious theory was that he was the one trying to slow down the trial by having members of the jury murdered.

But Wiley's relief when the judge concluded that he was associated with the element of water, and the sub-house of salt water within that, was odd. Ty was sure that something else was going on below the surface.

He had no idea what that might be, but there were deeper secrets to uncover if they wanted to find out what was really going on. Kennedy's statement that he was being framed haunted him. Granted, he could have just said that to make the jurors sympathetic, but somehow Ty didn't think so.

The solution definitely wasn't as easy as Judge Fathom seemed to think.

He parked the car in a visitor's spot and killed the engine.

"Wow, this place is a lot bigger than I thought." Finn stared at the converted warehouse—well, that's what it appeared as to civvies—at the edge of India Basin.

"You've never been?" Ty led the way to reception, his slightly more resistant prisoner still in tow.

"Never had a reason to come here." Finn shrugged "Haven't been in the area that long, anyway."

"True." Ty thought that Bermuda was a much nicer place to live, and that Finn would probably want to return there as soon as the trial was over. Why did that make him feel so empty? He hardly even knew the man.

They were asked to take a seat while someone tracked Julian down and got an officer to book the prisoner.

Five minutes later, the receptionist informed them that Julian was nowhere to be found. Apparently he was working on an undercover case and wasn't expected to return his calls until sometime during the night. At least she gave him the correct number to use to leave a message.

Great.

A young female officer, straight out of the academy, came up to them to book Wiley. The bastard left with a grin on his face. Ty didn't trust him as far as he could throw him. He had a very bad feeling about this.

He walked back to reception, Finn in tow, as soon as Wiley and the young officer had vanished around a corner. "I need to make some confidential phone calls. Is there a meeting room I can use?"

He was given a room number and directions. The security check they had to undergo to get there was just as harrowing as any others he'd been through. At least he got to keep his gun after having it checked.

Finn looked bored the entire time Ty was making his phone calls, but he wasn't going to let him out of his sight. If whoever was behind this was able to get a murderer into a courtroom, not even the police station was safe. He wasn't ready to risk Finn's life for anything.

Half an hour later, with enough messages left and promises made to reassure him that Julian would be able to take over the case, they finally left the police station for his home in Redwood.

After one detour to Fabulous Cupcakes to pick up some new healing cakes, they finally arrived at his refuge. Ty was as happy to be home as ever, and having Finn with him once again was just the icing on the cupcake.

"Takeout okay?" He unlocked the front door then entered, carefully balancing the box of cupcakes Easter Sunrise had put together for them and putting them on the kitchen counter for later consumption. "It's still early, but I'm kinda hungry."

"You know me." Finn grinned as he got them each a bottle of beer. The man moved around the kitchen as if he lived in this house. It was nice.

"Yeah, I'm beginning to." Ty grinned back and pulled the takeout menus from their designated drawer. "You're always hungry."

"Yep." Finn plopped himself onto the sofa in the living room, open beer bottle at the ready. "I wouldn't mind Thai tonight."

"Thai, let me see…" He leafed through the menus.

"Only if you're okay with it." Finn looked worried.

"Look, you've had a tough day, almost getting killed again, so you get to choose what you want to eat…whether you like it or not." Ah, there they were. He pulled the colourful brochures he wanted from the stack. "And anyway, Thai is only my favourite food, so it's not exactly a hardship for me to have some."

"Really?" Finn's eyes lit up, expressing relief and joy all at the same time.

Ty nodded, his throat suddenly too tight for speech. And someone wanted to kill this wonderful man? He swore, yet again, that he was going to do everything in his powers to find and stop those responsible.

Once he'd ordered enough food to feed two starving men, he returned to the sofa and sat down next to Finn. The man was simply breathtaking. He was a little tense now, but that was something he could remedy.

"Why don't you put up your feet for a bit, just until the food arrives?" He put his empty beer bottle on the low table. Then he began rubbing his hands together to relax them, get them warmed up and ready for what he planned to do to Finn.

"Yeah?" Finn raised his eyebrows and smiled when he nodded. "That sounds good, actually."

Ty helped him lie lengthwise on the sofa, feet propped up on one of the arms. He carefully took off the elegant leather loafers, wondering what Lilly at Fabulous Cupcakes would have to say about them. They were quickly followed by the socks. Ty glanced up at Finn who lay back with his eyes closed and already seemed half asleep.

"Pants, too." He kept his voice low in case Finn really was asleep. He didn't want to wake him.

Finn's eyes flew open. "You want me to take off my pants?"

"It'll be easier for you to relax that way." Clearly, he'd also have a better view, but that was secondary. Probably.

Finn raised his eyebrows, but the little twinkle in his eyes and the relative haste with which he took off his pants confirmed that his shock couldn't have been too real. When he lay back down again, boxers neatly covering his bits, Ty let his gaze wander along the long, lightly furred legs. They were a work of art. The muscles showed a runner's strength...or maybe a swimmer's? They were so well-formed that he just knew he could spend hours staring at them.

Carefully keeping his gaze away from the tempting—and not inconsiderable—bulge at Finn's crotch, he focused on the man's feet.

Even they were beautiful.

Strong, long and with perfectly shaped toes, they simply drew his hands. He wanted to kiss them. Later.

He stroked the top of each foot first, using both hands simultaneously. Moving from toe to ankle, he made his touch strong enough to feel, following with the same kind of touch on the sole of Finn's feet. When he increased the pressure, Finn moaned and relaxed more deeply into the sofa.

The moan went straight to his balls and made his cock stir. *Down boy.* This was about Finn.

Focusing on the right foot first, he made circular movements with his thumb and fingers, moving from the top and working his way down. When he touched the sides, Finn moaned again. Gritting his teeth for control, he started working the toes, rolling each between his thumb and forefinger as he slid his fingers towards the end. He carefully repeated the circular motions along the sole then changed to stroking the sole and instep again before giving the same treatment to the left foot.

When he was done, he was hard. Looking up, he saw Finn move his head up to look at him. He blinked a few times until he finally looked at Ty with glazed eyes.

"That was amazing." Finn smiled and sank back into the sofa. "I just need a nap now and I'll be fine."

Regretfully, that was exactly what Ty had planned for Finn—to give him the maximum amount of rest before their food arrived. However, that had been before he knew how exciting a foot massage could be...not just for the recipient. Manfully sticking with his chivalrous intentions, he pulled a soft blanket from one of the chairs and covered Finn.

When he bent down to kiss his cheek, he was surprised to feel the man snake his arm around his middle to pull him down onto the sofa.

"Join me?" Finn's voice sounded drowsy, already half asleep.

Crawling under the blanket with Finn now that he had an invitation was a no- brainer. Figuring out how to position himself so that his hard erection wouldn't poke Finn in the side was impossible.

"Okay." Finn tightened his grip around Ty's middle, shifting his hand down until Ty could feel him grip an ass cheek. Finn pulled until Ty had no choice but to press his groin into the other man's hip. "Hmm, nice."

"Yeah." He agreed with that, even though it was very difficult not to move and hump Finn's thigh.

"We'll have to do something about it in a little while." Finn chuckled and wiggled a little until their bodies fit together perfectly. "When I feel less drowsy."

"All right." Who was he to reject an offer like that? He could only hope Finn would remember what he'd said once he woke up.

Finn turned his head and blinked his eyes open again. It looked like hard work.

"Kiss goodnight?"

Oh man, he was so lost. Moving his head closer to Finn's, he brushed their lips together and pulled back. Finn was having none of it.

Bringing up his other hand, Finn slid it around the back of his head and pulled him close.

"Now kiss me like you mean it."

Demanding much?

Ty had no reason to fight Finn, so he gave in. This time their lips locked together as if that was their natural state of being. Nibbling and licking the outside, then plunging his tongue into Finn's hot mouth to explore his depths, Ty was overwhelmed with the strong flavour that greeted him. Deep like the ocean and with as many layers as a coral reef, Finn's mouth proved to be the perfect place to explore. Maybe spend the rest of his life in.

When their tongues met and caressed each other, his excitement rose to the next level. Finn was so responsive—he started to move his body against Ty's. The wavelike stimulation across the entire length of his body drove his arousal ever higher until he needed air desperately enough to enable him to pull back.

Panting for oxygen, they both wore goofy grins on their faces.

"Wow." Finn smiled. "Who knew?"

"Yeah." Too exhausted to figure out what that meant, he filed it away for later analysis.

"Nap."

Finn just nodded against the side of his neck and started snoring softly.

Ty blinked.

That was an amazing achievement.

Ty closed his eyes and let himself drift off. The food delivery guy was sure to wake them. That would be soon enough to return to reality. For now, he would enjoy Finn's arms around his body and being able to bury his nose in the other man's chest to breathe in his musky scent.

This was even better than Thai food...

Chapter Four

Finn awoke to a shrill-sounding doorbell. He was on a soft, flat surface, but it didn't feel like a bed. Someone with a very hard body, pressing against him in all the right places, had his arms around him, making him feel all warm and cuddly. It was nice, but where was he and who was the hunk next to him who stirred, but didn't seem to want to wake up? He was so disoriented, it took him a few more seconds to figure it out.

Then it all came back to him. The second attempt on his life. Ty going all protective, setting in motion the investigation ordered by Judge Fathom. The suspicion that something bigger than King Neptune wanting to stop his youngest son's trial was going on. Their trip to the police station and, eventually, back here to Ty's house. Oh God, that heavenly foot massage Ty had given him followed by the hottest make-out session he'd experienced in his life.

Too bad they'd both been so exhausted. He would have loved to find out what else they could do to each other's bodies besides kissing. The thought alone had him half hard and wanting to wake up Ty to see what they could come up with.

The doorbell shrilled again, more insistently this time. What a horrible sound. More suited to raising the dead than alerting them that someone was at the door. Why did Ty have such an ugly-sounding doorbell? More to the point, who the hell could be so insistent as to keep ringing it?

Food!

That was a reason to get up. Ty still wasn't moving other than to breathe and grumble a little at the disturbing sound, so Finn extricated himself from the embrace and finally rose from the sofa. He didn't want the delivery guy to leave with the food and have them starve.

He opened the door and was faced with a young girl, loaded with several bags of very Thai-smelling food. One sneaker-shod foot was tapping an impatient rhythm against the porch floor and her bubble gum popped right when he was about to say hello, the blonde ponytail bouncing in response.

"I've got a delivery from Bamboo Garden for a Mr. Anglin?" She looked him up and down as if she could confirm his identity by checking him out. Her eyes widened in shock when she reached his legs.

What? Were his pants dirty or something? He looked down. *Oh shit.* He wasn't wearing any. Too intent on opening the door and getting their food he'd forgotten to put them back on. He shrugged. Nothing he could do about it now, she was going to have to deal.

"I'll take that." He reached for the bags.

"That'll be thirty-two fifty." She handed them and the bill over, still eyeing him warily.

"Give me a moment." Not wearing any pants, unfortunately there wasn't any money on him, either. Was he going to turn around to let her have a good look at his butt? Was that going to get him more arrested than just standing there in his boxers and not moving?

"Here you go, Miss." Ty's long-fingered hand reached past him, handing a bundle of notes to the stunned girl. "Keep the change."

The girl grabbed the money, barely looking at it to make sure there was enough. She turned around and ran for the delivery van, escaping the craziness that was her latest set of customers as fast as she was able.

"Thank you." Finn closed the door and turned around to give his decently pants-wearing saviour a kiss. "I've always wanted to be rescued by a Marshal."

"Rescued from that girl's advances or from being arrested for inciting a riot due to exposure of gorgeous legs?" Ty grinned mischievously as he carried the bags into the kitchen.

"Advances?" He hadn't noticed any of those, thank God. He wouldn't have known where to look.

"Yeah, she was looking awfully interested." Ty got some paper napkins and hesitated over the cutlery. "Modern or traditional?"

"Oh, I'm a traditional guy myself." Finn licked his lips just thinking about watching Ty eat with his fingers. He hoped lots of licking would be involved. The thought alone had him half hard.

Ty quirked an eyebrow as he got the required chopsticks for the noodle soup. He pointed at the fridge. "Get us some beers, will you?"

"And no way was that girl interested in me. She was probably just shocked. I really should have put my pants on before answering the door." He got two more bottles of beer, held them up to Ty—who nodded—then opened them and followed the other man back into the living room.

"Yeah, you should have." Ty laughed as he set the bags onto the low table and started to pull out all the little boxes, opening and smelling each one. "Sorry about leaving you to it. I can't believe I slept that hard. I've never missed something like a phone call or the doorbell before."

Especially with that God-awful doorbell sound of yours. But he didn't say anything. Maybe the man was attached to it for some reason?

"It's no problem—you were there when it counted." The longer he thought about it, the more relieved he was about the rescue.

Finn grinned and they started digging into the food. Literally. The crispy wheat noodles in sweet chicken curry soup was wonderful and Ty handled the chopsticks like a natural. Then came the fun part. As tradition demanded—before vice-king Pinklao decided to Westernize Thai eating etiquette in the eighteen-fifties—they used their right hands to eat the rice, dunking it into the various curries. It was great fun, if somewhat messy. They were soon feeding each other, their looks getting more heated by the minute. Licking Ty's fingers as he took another morsel from him was almost as much fun as Ty licking back.

Man, Ty had a mouth like a vortex. The suction was strong enough to keep him hard. Thinking of that mouth on other parts of his anatomy was extremely stimulating. He tried to focus on the food—he really did—and it was excellent. The coconut curry held his interest for a while, the stir fried chicken with ginger made him sit up and notice, and the fried rice noodles with tofu were to die for.

Before he knew it, he was too stuffed to move, and Ty was still eating. Where did he put all that food? There wasn't an ounce of fat on the man's body. He looked at his somewhat sticky fingers, wondering idly where to find the energy to get up and clean them more thoroughly.

"Let me take care of that for you." Ty winked at him.

"More licking?" He could so deal with that.

"Better."

What could be better than licking?

He helped clean away the little food that had remained. Ty gripped his hand, securely sticking their fingers together then pulled him up the stairs. He followed the other man into his bedroom — which he barely had time to notice was decorated in hues of blue and green — then his bathroom.

He tried not to let his jaw drop. Water was definitely this man's element. Blue marble tiles lined the floor — white ones, the walls. A sunken bathtub that looked more like a grotto was in one corner, a huge shower with several heads sat in another, enclosed by glass doors. There were two green marble wash basins with shell-shaped soap holders, several mirrors and a continuous waterfall coursing down one of the walls. The faucets and towel racks were golden. A huge window let in enough light to make everything sparkle.

"You like?" Ty's eyebrows rose.

"I love!" He looked around again, making sure he hadn't missed anything. He didn't even know where to start.

"Come on, I think we need a shower." Ty had made the decision for him.

Once Ty had turned on the water, they both got undressed. He didn't have that much to take off, so when he was done, he was just in time to watch Ty take off his pants. Strong, well-formed calves and thighs guided his gaze upwards to the huge package. His mouth started to water as Ty removed his briefs, standing tall and proud under his gaze. Oh yeah, washing that body was not going to be a hardship.

Ty held out his hand and led him into the shower. The warm water felt wonderful on his tired muscles and he tilted his head back under the spray nearest to him, closed his eyes and relaxed. The soft closing of the shower door barely registered but the well-soaped hands on his chest a few moments later definitely did. He smiled to let Ty know it was okay, but kept his eyes closed as the other man soaped him up. Ty paid special attention to Finn's fingers, massaging his arms and gradually moving farther down to clean his cock and balls, then his ass.

When Ty was done, Finn opened his eyes to return the favour. Touching this hot man's body all over was extremely arousing. When he was done with the rest, he slowly stroked Ty's fingers clean.

"I need to kiss you now." Ty's voice was low and rumbled straight into his heart.

"Sounds good to me."

He stepped into Ty's open arms and slid his own around the other man's slim waist. Holding on to the delectable ass cheeks was going to be at least half the fun. Tilting his head to get just the right angle, Ty moved closer and touched their lips together. A current of desire and arousal raced straight into his cock and made him harder than he'd already been from the thorough cleansing.

Tongues duelling and hands roaming everywhere they could reach, he pushed closer until their cocks were aligned just so. Slowly rocking against Ty's body provided delicious friction that soon increased his arousal to the point where he needed more. He pushed closer still until Ty stopped moving.

Finn blinked his eyes open for a second.

The wall was now holding them up. *Good*. If their kissing so far was any indication, they'd need all the support they could get. He moved his hands up to stop them from being squashed against the tiles and used them to hold onto Ty's shoulders instead. Even they were muscular and strong enough to inspire trust.

Returning to the matter at hand, he kissed Ty for all he was worth. The other man gave as good as he got, returning each caress and every touch with intoxicating enthusiasm. Finn was so turned on, he didn't know what to do next. All he wanted was to be close to Ty, and since crawling inside him didn't seem to be an option, he ground his hips into the other man's groin as hard as possible while continuing to caress every nook and cranny in his mouth with his tongue.

The dark flavour of the man's kisses and the feel of his hands kneading Finn's ass cheeks and stroking his back added to the scent of the sea-salt based shower gel they'd used, providing a level of sensory stimulation that had him needing to come within minutes. He deepened the kisses as he pushed his hard cock against Ty's skin and focused on finding relief.

Seconds later the tingling in his balls signalled he was close. His hips' movements turned erratic, his entire body stiffened and he let go in waves of pulsing pleasure that had him seeing stars. Ty groaned and more heat splashed up between them as Finn followed him over the edge.

They both shook with the force of their orgasms and Finn put his forehead on Ty's shoulder for support while he caught his breath. Being held like this, warm water lightly spraying them from above and listening to their harsh breathing as it slowly returned to normal, made him feel better than he had in many years. It almost felt as if he belonged here…with Ty.

After a while they'd both regained enough of their strength to turn off the water, towel themselves dry and make their way over to the largest bed Finn had ever seen. Ty pulled back the dark green bedspread and started to climb in.

"You coming?"

"You want me to stay here?"

"Unless you prefer the cold, lonely guestroom…" Ty smiled as he patted the mattress next to him. "I'll bet you'll sleep better next to me. It'll be a lot safer as well."

Truth be told, that's where he wanted to be. His safety wasn't really an issue, since he was staying at Ty's house where nobody suspected he'd be. But as long as it gave him an excuse to stay close to Ty, he certainly wasn't going to complain.

So he nodded and got in, snuggling up against Ty. Yeah, this was much better than the small double he'd slept in last night. This was where he was going to stay from now on if he had anything to say about it.

* * * *

The Water Court didn't look any different than it had the day before. Most of the jurors were already seated in their shell-like chairs, the court watchers were busy chatting up a flood, and the number of bailiffs watching over everybody looked to be about the same as yesterday.

Ty still walked in with a feeling of foreboding that hadn't been there before the most recent attempt on Finn's life. The revelations about a potential conspiracy behind the Camelot trial, not to mention the extreme irregularity of an assassin actually making it into a court of law, disturbed him.

Staying close to Finn just in case there was another attempt on his life had become more than his job over the last twenty-four hours. He'd never fallen for a client before, but since they were both consenting adults, he didn't really feel bad about it, per se. He just hoped there wouldn't be any complications later on.

Luckily, Julian had called back the previous night — well, in the middle of the night to be exact — to let him know that he'd be taking the case. Apparently his superiors had already made sure his undercover job, which he'd only started actively working on the day before, would be taken over by a colleague. The importance of the Kennedy investigation, as it had been dubbed, was high enough for several people in the superpowers police hierarchy to make some exceptions.

A quick briefing over the phone had enabled him to make a start, but Ty wasn't sure how much his old friend could do with so little information. All they really had was an assassin, Wiley Tritos, who might or might not reveal who had hired him. They also had a list of suspects a mile long, since anyone in the royal family could have hired Wiley. They would all benefit to some degree — although the king's interest, as a father and as a monarch, was probably the highest.

He hoped the judge would give them some time for at least the preliminary investigation to start looking into who might be behind the removal and attempted removal of jurors. Whoever it was apparently lacked any fear of legal repercussions. The punishment for interference in elemental superpowers law was severe, and generally applied as ruthlessly as it was to unsanctioned superpowers interference in human lives and affairs.

Reluctantly, he let Finn take his seat in the jury box. Keeping an eye on the rest of the court room occupants would be the bailiffs' job. Ty would make the officials his primary observation target.

He sat down as close to the jury box as possible, just in case. Taking one of the bailiffs' seats just under the judge's raised desk was a bit irregular, but he didn't care. He'd not only be at Finn's side more quickly if needed, but he also had a good view of the entire room and all its occupants.

Robert Hydros, the water lawyer working closely with Ephyrus Bainbridge, was worth keeping an eye on. The young lawyer's smug smile following yesterday's interruption of the court session was suspicious. Ty wanted to know what he'd found so satisfying about the trial being stopped. By all rights, the prosecution should be worried about that.

Brian Pontus, the defence lawyer, was under automatic suspicion. He should have been the one most interested in stopping the trial, if the rumours of the royal family's displeasure were to be believed. Strangely enough, he'd only been concerned about Kennedy's state of emotional distress at being returned to custody so unexpectedly.

Finally everyone was seated—the chair next to Finn conspicuously empty for the time being—and only Judge Fathom was missing. As far as Ty was concerned, he couldn't get here quickly enough.

An hour later the judge still hadn't appeared and Ty, along with everyone else in the courtroom, was ready to climb the walls.

Two hours later than expected, the door to the judge's chambers suddenly opened, and Judge Fathom stepped out. He looked slightly dishevelled, the hand still running through his thinning hair somewhat explaining that condition. The judge looked around the courtroom, his gaze resting slightly longer on the prosecution's table, before he sat down in his chair.

He looked entirely too rattled for Ty's peace of mind.

"This court will come to order." The judge banged his gavel three times as tradition demanded. "The trial of Superpowers versus Mr. Kennedy is now in session."

Complete silence greeted the judge's announcement.

"There have been some new developments." The judge rubbed his temples before forcing his hands back down onto the bench in a clear attempt to appear relaxed. "In light of the new information that was brought to my attention within the last hour, the trial will be suspended until further notice."

What?

Ty was no lawyer, but even he was pretty sure that this was unprecedented. Shocked looks all around were proof enough that nobody had expected this.

Finn and the other jurors sat with their mouths open.

The lawyers also looked shocked, Mr. Hydros a little more so than the others. His skin tone hovered closer to green than white as he swayed in his seat before he pulled himself together and sat still, staring at the judge in open horror.

The court watchers and other attendees' reactions ranged from gleeful to curious to just as shocked as the officials'.

Complete bedlam was the next stage, as everyone started to talk at the same time. Ty closed his eyes for a moment, trying to figure out what this meant for Finn and him. Was the danger now gone or would it get worse? There was no way to know until they found out what the judge planned to do about some of the issues still pending. Better yet, they needed to find out what this 'new information' the judge had referred to consisted of.

"Order." The judge didn't have to raise his voice to be heard. He'd used his Water-Power to make it resonate straight into everyone's brains.

"There are two statements I wish to make at this point in time." The judge looked around as if to make sure everybody was listening. "First, the selection of a new member of the jury will start immediately. It is my understanding of the current situation that the trial will continue as soon as some key pieces of information have been found and confirmed. Therefore, we will need a full jury to stand ready as soon as we can proceed."

The journalists seated at the back of the audience area were furiously taking notes. Mr. Bainbridge looked happy whereas Mr. Hydros looked increasingly worried. The defence lawyer frowned, probably still trying to figure out what this meant for Mr. Kennedy.

"The second statement I wish to make is related to the reason for my delaying the opening of this session." Judge Fathom sighed. "It has been brought to my attention that there is additional information about the murders of jurors Nancy Sugarman and Hill

Jacobs, as well as the two separate incidents of attempted murder of Mr. Garrison, I might add. While this evidence is new and still uncorroborated, the facts presented to me have convinced me that a more detailed investigation is warranted. This requires time, and since the outcome will determine the future of this case, we cannot sensibly proceed until a final report is available."

Shit!

Julian must have discovered some really heavy-duty stuff for it to have such an impact. Looked like his theory about something bigger going on behind the scenes had to be correct. *Go Julian!*

A few more seconds of stunned silence were followed by complete chaos. Some of the journalists rushed out of the room, presumably to make reports to their headquarters. Mr. Bainbridge was frowning and Mr. Hydros looked positively panicked until he noticed Ty looking at him and schooled his features into a mask of indifference. *Interesting.* Mr. Pontus just shook his head and started collecting his paperwork to return it to his briefcase.

The judge turned towards the jury.

"As previously instructed, you are not to discuss this case with anyone. Each of you will be provided with personal security until such time as this trial can resume. You will not leave the city without informing the court." Judge Fathom tilted his head. "Is that understood?"

All eleven members of the jury nodded, none of them looking happy.

"Mr. Anglin, I expect you to continue your duties as Mr. Garrison's bodyguard, as well as to support Detective Julian Narragan in his investigation. Will that be a problem?" The judge's facial expression made it clear he didn't expect there to be.

"No, Your Honour, that will not be a problem." In fact, he couldn't wait to get started. He hadn't been involved in such an interesting investigation in a long time, and given that he could still protect Finn at the same time, he looked forward to it.

* * * *

"So, Julian, what have you got for me?" Ty walked into his old friend's office, a big smile on his face.

"Ty, it's good to see you." Julian rose from behind his cluttered desk so they could hug. "And who is this gorgeous guest you've brought me?"

"Now, now, I haven't brought him for you." In fact, he'd do whatever necessary to keep Julian well away from Finn, if Julian was this interested. "This is Finn Garrison, one of the jurors in the Kennedy trial. He's under my special protection."

"Oh he is, is he?" Julian grinned, making full use of his boyish charm as he turned towards Finn. "It's a pleasure to meet you."

"Same here." Finn looked decidedly unsure as he shook the detective's hand.

"Please have a seat. Would you like some coffee or something?" Julian pointed at two visitors' chairs in front of his desk. "We may be here for a while."

"Yes, please, coffee would be good." Ty sat, moving his chair closer to Finn's. If his urge to stay close at all times hadn't been so strong, it might have been embarrassing. As it was, he had no doubts it was right, and bore Julian's raised eyebrow with equanimity.

"For me too, please." Finn glanced at him, a small smile forming on his lips.

Had the man figured him out? Or did he feel the same way?

Julian called his secretary, asking for three coffees, then leant back in his chair.

"Before we get started with the details, let me just say that I'm pretty sure this is going to be one of the most interesting cases of my career as a Water Detective so far." Julian's eyes twinkled and he looked to be in his element as he shuffled some of the papers into slightly neater stacks.

"Really?" Finn raised his eyebrows. "I didn't know finding a murderer and getting a confession out of him would be this fascinating."

"Oh, you have no idea. If my initial findings are correct, this is a lot more than a simple murder investigation. We may have apprehended the suspect, but the suspicion of someone else being behind the murders seems to be correct." Julian rubbed his hands. "Proving this and getting them stopped and arrested will be far more interesting."

"So Wiley Tritos didn't act on his own?" Ty smiled. "I knew you were the right guy for this case."

"Well, like I said, we haven't got any definitive proof yet, but—" Julian looked at the door when a knock sounded, frowning slightly. "Come in."

A middle-aged woman wearing a straight skirt and a white blouse walked in and placed a tray with a carafe of coffee and three sets of cups and saucers onto Julian's desk. The superpowers police force was nothing if not civilised. Ty grinned.

"Will there be anything else?" The secretary stepped back, making sure she didn't run into any of the filing cabinets lining the wall.

"Not for now, Sally, thanks." Julian smiled as she nodded and backed out of the office, closing the door on her way out.

The coffees were quickly distributed and for a few moments the only sounds in the room were those of quiet sipping and some relieved moans as the caffeine started to work. Ty had no idea what he'd do without coffee in his life.

"Right, now that we've dealt with all the interruptions, can we *please* get to the point?" Finn put down his coffee cup and looked at Julian. "You were saying that you have a theory about the person behind the murders of two jurors?"

"Yes, I do." Julian leant back in his chair, put his elbows on the armrests and steepled his hands in front of him. "More than a theory—we have a statement from Mr. Tritos."

"That was quick!" Ty couldn't believe it.

"Did you torture him or something?" Finn looked horrified.

"No, we certainly did not." Julian growled. "Even if we had, torture usually takes time to take effect, and all we had was less than twelve hours from the time I received Ty's message."

"So, what did you do and who is behind it?" Ty gritted his teeth to try to contain his impatience. Julian was certainly drawing this out longer than necessary.

"We used an old and little known form of Water Power called Flushing." Julian looked smug. "It's useful when you want a suspect to reveal his motives or make a confession and don't have a lot of time to do it in."

"Flushing?" Ty scrambled to remember the details of his Water Power studies.

"It's a non-invasive technique using a special type of algae and a Water Mage's talents. It literally flushes all of a suspect's memories into a rare type of coral, from where the Water Mage can retrieve details related to specific events. This has to be done quickly because the coral can only hold the memories for a short time before they evaporate and return to the original owner." Finn shrugged. "It's not knowledge available to the general superpowers population."

"For good reason," Ty remembered now. "It's not without its dangers for the participants, if I remember correctly."

"No, it isn't." Julian nodded. "We only use it very rarely and it needs a judge's approval."

"Hence, the long delay this morning. I was wondering why it took you so long to inform the judge of the new situation. You were actually getting his permission to perform the procedure, weren't you?" Ty leant forwards when Julian nodded. "Now that we know how you did it, we obviously want to hear what you found out."

"It wasn't anyone within the royal family, nor anyone even remotely connected to them." Julian grinned.

"No?" Ty was truly shocked. "But they're the ones who'd benefit from the trial not continuing."

"Maybe." Julian nodded. "But based on what we know now, they weren't involved. They may ultimately benefit from it, but they weren't behind these attempts. And there are other people—other groups—who'd be happy if the trial were stopped."

"Who?" Finn looked doubtful.

"According to Mr. Tritos, he was paid by Louis Hydros." Julian smiled.

"Louis Hydros? From the Hydros family?" Ty found that hard to believe, but Julian nodded for emphasis. "The same Hydros family that the assistant prosecutor, Mr. Robert Hydros, is part of?"

"One and the same." Julian still hadn't moved other than to nod.

"Okay, hold on here." Ty raised a hand. "You're saying that someone in the Hydros family paid Wiley Tritos to kill jury members and slow down the trial."

Julian nodded.

"But the Hydros family has a strong interest in getting Mr. Kennedy convicted. Why would they want to slow down the trial?" Ty scratched his head.

"Because getting Mr. Kennedy convicted isn't as important to them as discrediting the royal family. That conviction would have helped — and was part of the plan — but as far as I understand the situation now, they believed that accusing the royal family of murder, making it look as if they were killing jurors, would be even more effective." Julian sighed. "And, ultimately, they assumed nobody would ever discover their involvement."

"So, let me get this straight." Ty's head was beginning to hurt. "The Hydros family wants the royals to be discredited? Why?"

"That's the part which, so far, is only a theory. And it's one with a few holes to fill, let me tell you." Julian lowered his hands, shifting in his chair. "But, best as I can figure it, there's an old family feud between them. The Hydros family and their powers are linked to fresh water, whereas the royal family, including the family of the defence lawyer, Mr. Pontus, is linked to salt water."

"And?" Finn's face was scrunched up in thought.

"Fresh water families, just like their power source, are a minority. Apparently, a long suppressed minority now wanting their rights." Julian shrugged. "I had no idea this was going on and we need to dig deeper so we can understand it, but on the surface of it, with salt water making up ninety-eight per cent of the Earth's water supply, the one thing that is certain is the minority status of the fresh water families within the Water House."

"But why would that be a problem?" Ty shook his head. "I've never even heard about discrimination or suppression between the Water Houses."

"Well, if it is a problem, and if they are planning a revolution of some kind, we need to find out more details." Finn pushed a hand through his hair. "This is definitely turning out to be a lot bigger than a murder trial. Not that even just the trial was ever simple, but with this additional information, at least some of the strange goings-on might have some sort of explanation. Mr. Kennedy may have been right when he said he was being framed."

"This is quickly turning into a major nightmare." Ty sighed and leant back, covering his face with his hands for a moment to try to focus. "We've solved two murders and two attempted murders of three members of the jury, only to discover a major conspiracy behind those murders. Possibly even behind the entire Kennedy trial."

"That about sums it up." Julian nodded.

What the hell was next?

Chapter Five

"Okay, so how are we going to do this?" Finn looked at Ty then Julian. "I guess we all agree that the official investigation needs to focus on Louis Hydros, who is the key suspect for setting up the juror murders and assassination attempts."

"Correct." Julian nodded. "Currently all we have is a statement from Wiley Tritos, so I'll need to focus on finding evidence. I also want to know *why* Louis Hydros did it. This may help us understand the bigger picture of what is behind the Camelot case. Hopefully it will also allow us to find some leads into this saltwater versus freshwater situation."

"That leaves the 'unofficial investigation' to us." Ty grinned.

"My thoughts exactly." Finn smiled.

How was it that they were thinking so much alike? It was great to have an ally, and he'd take any excuse to work with the gorgeous Water Marshal. Having him as a bodyguard was nice, though strictly speaking no longer necessary, since the assassin was now in custody. But at some point that assignment was going to end. He didn't want Ty to just vanish from his life. Spending more time with him on finding out what was going on would hopefully help them get to know each other better and maybe start building a relationship. God, he wanted that with an almost scary intensity.

"So, if Julian focuses on Louis Hydros, then we can try to find out why his brother Robert was acting so strangely in court." Ty frowned. "It's been bothering me for a while why the assistant prosecutor would be happy about a delay in the trial."

"And he was clearly happy." Finn shook his head. "I think it's just him, though, not the entire prosecution team. Mr. Bainbridge looked much more concerned."

"Which probably means you should check with him first." Julian tilted his head in thought. "He may or may not be aware of what is going on with his assistant lawyer, and he may be able to help us with this whole Water House situation."

"That's a good idea." Finn didn't like the thought of having to go and see the powerful lawyer, but they couldn't very well work around him either.

Once the decision had been made, they didn't delay. It was still early enough in the afternoon to pay Mr. Bainbridge a visit in his office, assuming that he'd give them an appointment on such short notice.

Ty wasn't worried and called the lawyer's office as they were walking to his car. Being a Water Marshal apparently had its advantages. Ty was immediately given an appointment. The drive across town was harrowing. Finn held on for dear life as Ty raced the Ferrari towards downtown at breakneck speed, leaving other cars behind as if they were water snails.

Finn was still trying to catch his mental breath when they arrived on the twelfth floor of the imposing office of Arden, Bainbridge, Chinook and Demek. All the partners' offices were located here—in fact, they seemed to take up the entire floor. The good-looking, young personal assistant in the anteroom to Mr. Bainbridge's office spared them a small smile before he announced their arrival to his boss.

"Send them right in, Barnaby." Mr. Bainbridge's voice carried well, even through the speaker system. "Make sure you offer refreshments as well."

"Certainly, sir." Barnaby clicked off the connection. He worked hard at suppressing a sour look in their direction but didn't quite succeed. "What can I get you, gentlemen?"

"I'd like some water, please." Ty grinned. "Shouldn't be a problem around here, should it?"

Barnaby nodded, his face now a mask of polite interest.

"Same for me please." Finn wondered briefly what Barnaby's problem was, then focused on the meeting ahead as they walked inside.

Mr. Ephyrus Bainbridge was clearly a powerful man. The office colours were deep blues and greens—the furniture and even window frames had been designed to reflect waves, spiralling vortices and drops of water. There wasn't a straight line in sight. Several aquariums lined the walls. A few touches of white here and there reminded Finn of foam on waves. The lawyer sat on a high-backed wicker chair behind a mother of pearl desk that dazzled with its brilliance. Papers and pens were strewn across it, forming haphazard, almost curly lines.

Mr. Bainbridge had sandy blond hair, which was just long enough to show the waves it might grow into if left alone. He smiled when he looked up.

"Please, have a seat." He waved at two very comfortable-looking canvas chairs which popped out of thin air and settled into the lusciously thick, dark blue carpet.

Finn hoped he wouldn't fall asleep. He had a tendency to nod off when relaxing at the beach, which was the only place he'd previously experienced a canvas chair. Barnaby interrupted his musings when he brought them two glasses of water, setting them on a mysteriously appearing small table between his and Ty's chairs. The personal assistant left without a backwards glance.

"Ah, the impertinence of youth." Mr. Bainbridge smiled. "Anyway, that is another story. What can I do for you?"

Finn cleared his throat.

"As you may have guessed, we're here in connection with the Camelot trial." Ty was trying to sit up straight, but the chair didn't make it easy. His facial expression, however, was all official Water Marshal now.

God, the no-nonsense look and slightly stiff body posture was such a turn on. All that was missing was his set of handcuffs. *Shit*. Finn wriggled in his chair — not an easy feat on a softly moving surface — to try to hide his hardening cock. They'd need some serious alone time soon. There were a few scenarios he'd like to give a try with this man. He'd never felt the urge to try bondage before, but somehow, the thought of being tied down by Ty — or maybe even tying him down — was more arousing than he'd ever thought possible.

"Indeed." Mr. Bainbridge leant back, steepling his fingers in front of him.

"We would like to ask you, in confidence, for your input and support regarding a part of the investigation which isn't quite official."

"Oh?" Mr. Bainbridge's eyebrows rose. "Nothing illegal I hope?"

"Sir!" Ty recoiled, looking horrified. "I'm a Water Marshal! There are certain standards to uphold and I am *very* aware of them."

"Just checking." The small movement of Mr. Bainbridge's lips, vaguely resembling a smile, was the only indication of his amusement. "May I hope that your request includes looking into the recent behaviour of my assistant on the Kennedy trial , Mr. Robert Hydros?"

Finn's mouth fell open.

Ty did a little better, covering up his surprise with a small frown as he nodded his agreement.

"Good." Mr. Bainbridge had a real smile for them this time. "It's more difficult for me to find out what's going on with him, at least without being obvious about it. And if my suspicions are correct, we need to be very, very careful."

"We do?" Finn's bad feelings about this whole situation deepened and the resultant sudden intense waves of anxiety made him dizzy. What the hell was going on if the powerful Mr. Bainbridge thought they'd need to be careful? What did he know and would he tell them? The nightmare of attempts on his life had been bad enough, but his intuition was telling him that the coming events might be far worse than that.

"Yes." Mr. Bainbridge nodded. "I can't tell you much, but from what little I can see, Robert has become involved with some very dark elements. Starting with his brother Louis, whom I suppose you'll be investigating fully?"

"How do you know about the role Louis allegedly played in this?" Ty narrowed his eyes. "That is not generally available information."

"It may not be, but I have my sources." Mr. Bainbridge got up and walked to the wall, pulling one of the sunken aquariums outwards to reveal a safe.

Huh? Finn was fascinated.

Mr. Bainbridge opened the safe, pulled a document out then closed the safe and replaced the aquarium where it belonged. Walking back to his desk, he handed the document to Ty before sitting down.

"What you have there, Mr. Anglin, is a list of names. They are people Robert Hydros has had meetings with over the last year or so. All of them are either political radicals, criminals or have otherwise caused the law to look into their affairs." Mr. Bainbridge rubbed his face. "I'm not sure what Robert is up to, but it cannot be good. I suggest you approach him with some sort of excuse and start looking into his affairs. My hands are tied, since I am his boss, and I cannot afford to draw attention to the fact that I'm suspicious due to my position in the firm."

"So you want me to investigate Robert Hydros?" Ty glanced at the document before pocketing it. "Why didn't you ask for help a long time ago? If, as you say, this has been going on for a while?"

"Quite frankly I didn't know whom to trust." Mr. Bainbridge leant forwards. "That, combined with the fact this has to be done quietly, meant that calling in a Water Marshal or even a detective wasn't possible without letting them know I was on to them. Now, with you coming to me in connection with the

Kennedy trial, we have a perfectly logical reason to have a meeting."

How devious was that?

* * * *

Finn couldn't wait to have a coffee or two and smother his sorrows in cupcakes. It was the next best thing crawling into bed with his Water Marshal and forgetting the world and all its conspiracies for a while. Getting some caffeine and food was, in fact, a prerequisite to doing anything else at all at this point.

It was early evening by the time they'd made it across town and were yet again entering the fantastic Fabulous Cupcake store. After the day he'd just had, he was in more than urgent need of some food for the soul. What better place to go than the superpowers bakery?

They entered the bakery side by side, only to be hit with an insane level of chattering, laughter and clinking of plates and utensils. The noise level was as unbelievable as ever. Daine, Christopher and Lilly were serving customers at the counter and two college kids were delivering orders to the lucky few who'd managed to grab a table. Everybody, including the ten or so elementals, seemed to be having a great time. The resulting chaos was amazing.

Why had he thought this would be a rejuvenating experience?

Christopher chose that moment to look up. His smile was bright enough to light up the room and Finn couldn't help but smile back. All he now felt for the dazzling Fire Mage was a deep friendship—the somewhat embarrassing attraction seemed to have dissipated. He reached for Ty's hand. Yeah, that was who he wanted.

"You okay?" Ty squeezed his hand but didn't let go.

"Yes, I think so." He looked at Ty and gave him the best smile he could find. "I really think I'm finally okay."

"You want to grab a table or should we go for takeout?" Ty looked around the room, seemingly dismayed with the lack of available seating.

"I'd love it if we could find a table…"

From the corner of his eye he saw Christopher stare, then point at a table for two in a relatively quiet corner. The couple suddenly got up as if their asses were on fire. Before he could think about it, he steered towards it, intent on reaching it before anyone else.

"Well done." Ty sat down and looked at him as if he'd been the one to perform the miracle.

"It wasn't me." He took his seat and grabbed the little menu.

"Never mind." Ty shook his head and focused on making a choice of food.

Finn waved at the harried college boy who was trying to run past instead of taking their order. With a small frown he stopped, pulled out his pad and smiled. It was a little forced, but under the circumstances, that was understandable.

"What would you like?" The boy tried to suppress a yawn.

Finn almost grinned. He remembered the times of too little sleep and too much partying. Thank God he was old enough not to want to do that anymore.

"I'd like a triple espresso to start with, followed by a large latte and whatever the cupcake special of the day is, please."

"A triple espresso as a starter?" The boy's eyes were wide enough they might fall out if he wasn't careful.

"Yes, please." Finn frowned. Maybe he was overdoing it and should change the order to a double. "Is there a problem with that?"

"No—no problem." The boy swallowed and turned to Ty. "And for you, sir?"

"I'll have a macchiato and the daily special as well, please." Ty returned the menu to its stand on the wrought iron table. "I'd also like a double chocolate delight with that."

The boy nodded, repeated the order in a shaky voice and ran off towards the counter.

"Looks like we shocked the poor kid." Finn grinned and leant back to survey the chaos. It looked a lot more manageable, comfortable even, now that they'd found somewhere to sit down.

"Never mind. I'm only interested in making sure we get our energy back. I've got plans for us later." Ty wriggled his eyebrows.

"Good, that seems to fit with what I was hoping for." He wriggled right back.

The laughter that followed was heartfelt and went a long way to relaxing him further. As long as he had Ty, coffee and cupcakes—in that order—he'd be fine despite whatever else the superpowers world threw at them.

"I brought you some samples." Christopher suddenly appeared at their table.

"What?" Finn jerked in surprise. Where had he come from?

"Oh, sorry, didn't mean to shock you." Christopher grinned and held out a little tray with some liqueur glasses, a tiny spoon next to each of them. Five glasses sat on the left, another five on the right. The colours ranged from white to pink, and the substance inside looked suspiciously like—He blanched and pulled back.

"Are you okay, Finn?" Ty looked worried once he managed to drag his eyes back open.

"Sure." He studiously avoided looking in the direction of the offending samples. "I just—just can't deal with those samples. Sorry Christopher."

"What? These small ones?" Christopher sounded surprised. "I'm sorry, I had no idea your aversion was this strong."

"What's going on here? What aversion? What's in those glasses? Is that why you're so pale?" Ty took his hand, drawing his attention away from Christopher's tray.

Christopher passed the tray to the female college student running by with yet another order on her notepad before he pulled up another chair and sat down next to them.

"Those were samples of a few new types of blancmange I want to try selling. Maybe in the pizza and pasta place next door once it opens, maybe even add them to the repertoire here. We'll have to see." Christopher sounded so excited. "I've been experimenting with different flavours for the sweet ones, infusing them with various healing properties from Easter Sunrise's store of flowers and herbs. The samples on the left were some new ideas for savoury varieties, such as chicken, mushroom, asparagus, aubergine and tomatoes. Thought they might make nice starters for next door."

Finn felt bad for having ruined the man's enthusiastic sharing of his new ideas.

"Those sound absolutely wonderful." Ty's eyes lit up. "I'd love to try them."

"Please go ahead, but could you do it out of my sight?" Finn shuddered just thinking about the consistency which was so much like Mr. Kennedy.

"You don't like blancmange?" Ty's eyes widened. "I didn't think that was even possible."

"I used to be just fine with it." Finn shrugged. "It's just that...to me, *you know who* in the court case looks too much like a blancmange for comfort."

"Is that what he looks like?" Christopher leant forwards. "That is amazing. It's definitely different from what legends say about his appearance."

"It is? What do you think could have happened to change him like that?" Finn had a strong feeling it had something to do with the whole reason for the court case.

"Well, from what I know about water monsters — and water elementals in general, for that matter — it's very rare for them to change appearance at all. Extreme temperatures can obviously do it, the most frequent influence being the cold of the far northern and southern reaches of Earth around the poles." Christopher tilted his head in thought. "I guess if you applied heat combined with some sort of other substance, you could go from a watery appearance to a blancmangey version."

"That almost sounds like an attack, or some sort of poisoning." Finn's eyes widened. "You think that's what might have happened to Mr. you-know-who?"

There was no point in mentioning his name here, where they could be overheard. The humans would think he was crazy and the elementals might panic.

"I don't know. I never thought about it that way, but you may be right." Christopher nodded.

"Another item we can add to our list of things to clarify." Ty rubbed his temples. "If this coffee and sugar overload isn't going to arrive soon, my head is going to explode."

"I'll go and see what's keeping them." Christopher got up, leaving them with one last smile.

Minutes later, the overworked college boy masquerading as a waiter approached with their food and drinks. The distribution was quickly made, and Finn dived for his triple espresso with embarrassing speed. He gulped the hot drink way too fast and it almost made him cough, but the positive effect of revival was worth a half-burned palate and tongue.

"Wow, you look like you needed that." Ty had already devoured half of his double chocolate delight cupcake.

"You're not much different with your chocolate fix, are you?" He laughed in pure relief at how much better he already felt. "I'm sure glad I'm not the only addict in this re…partnership."

"Uhm-hm." Ty was too busy munching on the other half of his first cupcake to respond.

Hopefully the man hadn't overheard his almost miss. It was way too early to talk about a relationship. Sheesh, they hadn't even known each other for a week yet. He was so pathetically needy. Finn wanted a partner so badly and things with Ty were so perfect — well, other than the murder and mayhem of the Kennedy trial. That didn't mean he should drop his guard like this, though. Maybe he'd been around Christopher and Marcel too much. Fire-people moved a lot faster than all the other elementals, except maybe the Wind-people. Those of the Water element definitely preferred a more leisurely pace than the one he wanted to go at with Ty. Damn it!

"Excuse me for interrupting your meal…"

Finn looked up, noticing from the corner of his eye that Ty was doing the same. None other than Brian Pontus, Mr. Kennedy's defence lawyer, was standing next to their little table, looking apologetic and much smaller than he did in court. He wore the same dark blue suit he'd had on that morning, but his dark hair was dishevelled and his glasses were slightly askew. He didn't look as relaxed as Finn would have expected. Shouldn't the fact that his client had a reprieve make him happy?

What the hell was he doing here anyway? It was most irregular for a defence attorney to approach a juror in a trial away from the courtroom. Finn began to panic. If anyone saw them talking, it could jeopardise the entire case.

"Are you mad?" Ty hissed. "You can't come to us-"

Pontus gave a dismissive wave of his hand. "The trial is suspended and I'll be brief."

Was there no peace and quiet for Ty and him anywhere? Wait...they weren't exactly in the right location for that. Fabulous Cupcakes was a great place, but not really conducive to enjoying quiet, private moments. Finn realised that Pontus had executed a Wave Order—a protective, watery bubble like a gigantic water blister around the three of them. It made their words echo and, in a, perhaps pleasurable side effect, produced feelings of euphoria in Finn.

He'd first discovered his own superpowers as a kid and the Wave Order had been his party trick. It always made him giddy, even when the subject turned serious. Covering his laughter with a cough, he raised his eyebrows at Mr. Pontus, inviting him to explain what he wanted.

The man seemed to find the giddiness contagious and suddenly giggled. He shook his head like a giant puppy shaking off water from a bath and harrumphed.

"Well, it's just that I saw you sitting here, and I was wondering if I could ask you a few questions." Mr. Pontus looked at Ty as he said this.

Ty raised his eyebrows, trying to swallow the last of his cupcake as he pointed at the chair Christopher had vacated minutes earlier.

"Thank you." Mr. Pontus sank down, the picture of relief. "I really appreciate this opportunity to talk to you...off the record, of course."

This was becoming interesting. Or rather, more interesting.

After the request for help from the prosecutor, now the defence lawyer wanted something from them as well? Maybe he'd better leave this one to Ty. After all, he was the Water Marshal here and would have a better handle on the legalities of the situation. Off the record or not, there might be consequences Finn couldn't even imagine.

"Okay, we can keep this off the record as long as whatever it is you want to discuss isn't illegal and won't interfere with my duties as a Water Marshal in general and my instructions regarding this case in particular." Ty had managed to finish his cupcake, wipe his mouth and have a sip of his macchiato as he was waiting for Mr. Pontus to decide if he still wanted to talk about whatever was bothering him.

"Of course, that goes without saying." Mr. Pontus raked a shaking hand through his hair and righted his glasses. "Okay, it's like this. As you may know, Mr. Garrison, my client has been saying that he's been framed from the very beginning. Unfortunately, the superpowers police had no interest in following up on his claim, since according to the detective in charge, there was no reason to look for evidence. The witnesses had made clear statements, they'd identified Mr. Kennedy and confirmed him as the suspect by the Water Mage in charge, and there was no indication any of them were wrong."

Ty nodded and finished his macchiato in one go.

"But, as bad a reputation as the royal family has in some circles, and as negative the image of water monsters in general—and of Mr. Kennedy specifically—they are not known for their capacity to lie." Mr. Pontus took a deep breath. "Obviously, I need to find out who framed my client and why. I suspect that only a powerful Water Marshal can get close to the truth in this case. Too many superpowers factions are fighting for territory here, and anyone who isn't extremely careful and knowledgeable might be in real danger."

It was a good thing Finn was a Water Mage, then. He wasn't about to let Mr. Pontus know, though. He had a feeling that it was better if they had at least one ace up their sleeves, so to speak...or did he know? How many people involved in the case knew that the three targeted jurors had been able to see Kennedy?

"I see no problem with that." Ty looked thoughtful. "I won't be able to run a full investigation, though."

"Obviously not, I understand that." Mr. Pontus nodded.

"What I can do is keep my eyes and ears open as I work on this case. If anything of use does come up, I will let you know."

"Thank you so much!" Mr. Pontus leapt up, catching the wobbling chair and stopping it from toppling over in the last second. "I don't want to keep you, but I really appreciate your help."

And with that, the man was off.

* * * *

Finn walked into Ty's house, beginning to feel truly at home here. His temporary bungalow on the beach at Half Moon Bay was all but forgotten, even though he probably could have moved back there now that the assassin had been captured. Not that he was going to bring it up with Ty. If the other man hadn't thought of it, Finn certainly wasn't going to rub his nose in it. He'd much rather spend more time with the handsome Water Marshal.

Closing and locking the door behind them as Ty went around switching on lights, he felt as if they'd done this for years. The muted colours, tasteful artwork, and luscious deep carpets included, held a warmth he'd never even felt in his home at Mermaid Beach. Thinking back, his own house seemed far away and kind of cold. The magnificent redwood building Ty had built with his own hands was becoming a true home with the two of them in it. He didn't even need his Mage's intuition to feel it.

"Nightcap?" Ty stood next to his small bar in the living room.

"Sure." He had some alternative ideas for a nightcap, but they could start with the more traditional approach. "Just nothing too alcoholic, please."

He wanted a clear head for the rest of the evening.

"How about a Blue Sapphire?" Ty grinned as he pulled a bottle of Blue Curacao from the shelf then took another from the small fridge.

"What is it?" He stepped closer.

"Just wait and see. It's really delicious, almost refreshing." Ty smiled. "That what you're looking for? Make sure we're both fit for what is to follow?"

He blushed, but nodded. Yeah, that pretty much summed it up. Judging from the growing bulge in Ty's pants, the other man wasn't exactly opposed to the idea.

Ty pulled two Collins glasses from another shelf, filled them with crushed ice then poured about an ounce of the blue liqueur into each of them. He filled the remainder with a red liquid that smelt like cranberry juice. Looked like it too — the colour was just that typical shade of bright red.

"There you go." Ty stepped closer and handed him a glass.

"Thank you." He looked across into Ty's hazel eyes which seemed almost green in the low light. Being pretty much the same height meant he didn't have to bend his neck to be able to make eye contact. It was very convenient when kissing, too.

Ty hadn't stepped back after handing him the glass and they touched elbows as they both took a sip from their drink. The proximity of his lover, the heady feeling of having the entire evening with him and the reviving abilities of the cocktail all combined into a mix of arousal that quickly had him well on the way to getting hard.

"You like it?" Ty grinned and downed half his drink at once, Adam's apple bobbing temptingly under his slightly stubbled skin.

"Oh, yeah." He loved everything about being this close to Ty.

"No, the drink." Ty grinned, finished his drink and put his glass away.

"Oh." He downed most of his own and put his glass next to Ty's on the sidebar. God, he wanted to kiss him.

Ty opened his arms as if on cue and Finn stepped right into them. Sliding his hands around Ty's middle, he let himself melt into the other man's body. Touching from groin to chest already felt pretty good. When Ty bent forwards to kiss him, his excitement mounted quickly. Licking and sucking each other's lips turned into caressing of tongues accompanied by roaming hands within seconds.

He could lose himself in these kisses.

"How far do you want to take this?" Ty had pulled back.

"As far as you want." He had no resistance where Ty was concerned — didn't even feel the need to try and keep his distance.

"A bed would be more comfortable for that." Ty grinned and started leading them towards the stairs.

Finn just nodded, admiring the muscles play under Ty's skin as he switched off the lights behind them. They were upstairs and undressed within minutes. Both being very motivated was a definite advantage. Once Ty had removed the bedspread, they tumbled onto the cool sheets and exchanged hot kisses as if their lives depended on staying lip-locked as long as possible.

Which turned out to be pretty long.

When they came up for air, Finn was hard enough to come within minutes. Ty's erection, pressed up against his hip, was in about the same state.

"Have you got stuff?" He didn't want to push Ty — at least not much — but he needed to move to the next stage. It had been a while for him, but he liked fingering himself as he let his hand do its thing, so it wasn't as if he needed major prep. He just wanted to feel Ty inside him.

Ty nodded, pulled lube and condoms from the drawer and deposited both in his hands. "Up to you."

He grinned as he unrolled the condom onto Ty's hard cock, making the other man moan and start humping the air. God, at this rate they were both going to explode before the main event. It was good to know his lover was versatile, but Finn knew what he wanted this first time. Grabbing the lube, he got himself ready, hissing at the sudden stretch.

Ty's eyes widened.

"Man, give me some warning next time. That's just too hot." Ty grabbed the base of his cock and squeezed—hard, from the look of it.

Without another word, he went to his hands and knees, looking back over his shoulder to see Ty's reaction. Ty moved so quickly, he was between Finn's spread legs and holding onto his hip with one hand in no time. Ty placed the swollen tip of his hard cock against his ass hole.

Then he paused.

"Please." Finn wanted it so badly.

"You want me to fuck you?" Ty pushed inwards a little then pulled back before he got anywhere close to where Finn wanted him.

"Yes!" He moaned when the hard cock finally entered him. The stretch was so much better than his fingers could ever provide.

"Shit." Ty's grip on his hip tightened and he grabbed hold with his other hand as well. "That feels amazing."

"Same here. Now stop talking and start moving." He was going to go out of his mind with want if Ty didn't move soon.

"Pushy, pushy." Ty's laughter sounded a little strangled — the man was still holding back.

"Never said I'd lay back and let you do what you wanted to me." He wasn't opposed — just the contrary. The thought of what use they could put Ty's handcuffs to made his arousal spike.

"No, you didn't." Ty laughed and that seemed to break the tension. "I just don't want to hurt you."

"You won't." He squeezed his ass muscles as he pushed back further, making his point. "But I might have to hurt you if you don't start moving soon."

"Got it." Ty pushed the rest of the way inside in one smooth move.

"Yes!" This was what he'd been looking for. That feeling of being utterly full...with the anticipation of being filled again and again as things progressed.

Ty pulled back, angling his cock in search of —

"Fuck!" There it was.

"Now we can." Ty thrust back inside at exactly the right speed and angle to make him scream with delight.

"Just like that."

Those were the last coherent words either of them spoke for a while.

Ty started fucking him as if he meant it, and the feeling of being stretched and filled again and again was amazing. Soft exhales of breath changed into moans then grunts of pleasure as Ty's thrusts became deeper and faster. He felt so close... His arms gave out and he sank to the bed. Pressing his forehead against the mattress, he reached back with one hand to stroke his cock. He needed the other for support to stop from being pushed into the headboard as Ty sped up.

"Close." He was ready to let go.

"Come for me." Ty's voice was rough and his movements lost their rhythm.

That voice and the unspoken need in it pushed him over the edge. He came in spurts of pleasure that raced through his entire body. Ty somehow kept up his thrusts until he was done. Only then did his lover let go, filling the condom as he trembled through his own orgasm.

Collapsing together after Ty had pulled out and cleaned them up a little, felt as natural as breathing. He closed his eyes, luxuriating in the feeling of being in Ty's arms. Everything else, at least for now, was suddenly a lot less important.

Chapter Six

Finn awoke, a sharp pain in his chest. He tried to move his head but something covered his face. He was suffocating! Something heavy was on him. He began to panic, pushing back against the thing sitting on him—a gigantic ass and belly...a glutinous but evil-eyed Buddha swamping him... Holy crap, it was the creature that had attacked him on the beach!

He had the sensation of sinking deeper and deeper into water. He tried to resist the creature's urge to drown him. Dear God, he was on the bed he'd shared with Ty, but he was on the verge of drowning. Fighting and kicking with everything he had, he heard a voice far away, echoing in his ears.

"Finn, Finn, it's only me. Stop it, you're hurting me!"

He screamed, "Help me!" His voice came out in a muffled strangle. Harking back to his childhood, he did the only thing a small, helpless kid would do. He bit the fat, watery ass trying to smother him.

Water broke from the slithery creature. It roared— the sound like something between a gigantic wave and a savage beast's wild howl. The water washing over him was rank and increasingly bilious with every bite. *Vile*.

Ty screamed, "Holy fuck! Finn!"

The fiend tried to roll away as Finn kept biting at the slimy ass shimmying on his face and body. Warm water kept erupting from the beast, escaping in pungent rivers into Finn's eyes and mouth. It was disgusting.

"I've got it," Ty shouted. "I've got the motherfucker. Holy shit, what the hell is it?"

Finn felt the creature rolling off him, but he had swallowed a lot of bile and could still hardly breathe.

"Roll over!" Ty shouted.

He rolled, heaving and coughing as the putrid green sludge poured out of him. Finn coughed and heaved and finally, though the taste was still horrifying and his eyes remained smeared and blurry, he reached for the phone.

"Who do I call?" he croaked. "Nine-one-one?"

Ty rattled off a phone number. "Tell him to hurry."

Finn kept trying to wipe his eyes so he could see, but even as poor as his vision was, he could see green ooze everywhere. Oh, crap, the bed was like a sea of slime. A naked Ty was on the bedroom floor, atop the monster that had attacked Finn. Its arms were being held behind it by Ty, who was struggling to secure restraints on it.

The call was answered.

"This better be good," said the deep gravelly voice on the other end of the line.

The monster roared and a swathe of green goo flashed across the bedroom wall. A fresh wave of the putrid stench made both Finn and Ty gag. With each fresh wound, the bile became more menacing.

"He said this better be good." Finn spat more bile as he called out to Ty.

"You tell that no good son of a gun, Amadis that he fucking *owes* me."

"Language, language," the voice said on the other end of the phone.

"We have a crisis." Finn cut into the man's amusement. "A creature tried to drown me in bed. I attacked it and Ty has it on the floor. He said to call you."

Ty gave a yell as the creature oozed more pus-like goo all over the floor.

"Fuck! Tell him to hurry."

"What is this creature?" Amadis asked with no hint of gravity or rush in his tone.

"I have no idea but it's big and fat and it sat on my face and I bit it and there's green, stinky ooze everywhere. I think it's the thing that attacked me on the beach a couple of days ago."

"Wait...*shit*...are you Finn Garrison?"

"Yes, I am." Finn started to cough uncontrollably. Good thing, too. It seemed his words had got through to the man on the other end of the phone.

"Is the creature secured?"

Finn glanced at Ty, still struggling with the behemoth. "Yeah. More or less. He's secreting a lot of fluids, but he's not getting any smaller."

"Ty's got him handcuffed?"

"Yes. He does, but man, the monster...he's still gigantic."

"You sure it's a he?"

"Yeah. I see a huge cock and balls."

"Okay, now describe his head."

Jesus, what's with the twenty questions?

"It kind of looks like a crown...a thorny crown."

"Is it green or purple?"

"Purple."

"Oh, God. Okay. Listen. You need to wash yourself as soon as you can. That's a fast-acting bile. It will eat through your skin. It's hard to treat."

Finn gulped in fear, taking in some of the bile. *Eew!*

"How many arms does it have?" Amadis asked.

How many arms? Finn's mind whirled as he glanced back at Ty.

Ty shouted, "Tell him two. It's just a baby."

"No need to repeat," Amadis said, his tone urgent now. "I heard. I'm on my way. You're lucky they sent a toddler. I'll be there in fifteen seconds."

Finn coughed, his chest and face burning.

"Hang up and get into the shower," Amadis barked. "Now!"

Ty held on to the baby Crown Thornslug, his legs and hands beginning to sting. The creature knew it was licked, and resorted to its best defence, sobbing and wailing like a baby.

"Not listening!" he shouted as the creature writhed underneath him, its face screwed up. It wouldn't work. He'd seen the real Thornslug's face and it was no sweet babe. It was a hideous sea monster.

"Amadis!" he yelled.

"You still have the hottest ass in Redwood City," a voice drawled behind him.

"Shut up and help me," he ground out.

"That's not nice. You woke me when I was in the middle of a very nice dream."

"Fuck you, Amadis."

"About...you."

"Oh, please. Come on, Amadis...help me. I'm on fucking fire here."

"Take it easy, man."

He heard the man's footsteps as he moved through the sludge and stood at the head of the creature. It stopped crying as Amadis took photos of it. The damned thing was smiling! Ty had never met a water creature yet that didn't have a massive ego. That included Amadis.

He watched Amadis withdraw a long ice pick from his coat pocket and stick it right into the monster's head.

The beast flattened out immediately, its bile going from green to silver, indicating death. Ty jumped to his feet. The silver bile was even more toxic than the green living bile.

"How did it get in?" Amadis asked. "This is supposed to be a secured building."

"You tell me," Ty said. "That's what I'd like to know." He walked towards the door. "I gotta take a shower and check on Finn."

Amadis said something, but Ty was over having any discussion with the guy. He stalked off to the bathroom, where he found Finn sitting on the bottom of the shower stall, arms around his knees, water running over him. He lifted his face to Ty's. It almost broke Ty's heart to see fresh bruises on the man's face.

"I'm sorry I hurt you," Finn said.

"Oh, Finn...please don't apologise. I'm sorry that thing hurt you. I'm sorry it ever got between us. I have no idea how it even got in here." He got into the shower and let the water run over him. The itching and burning stopped. Finn got to his feet, his hands running over Ty's body. He helped to wash the sludge from him, Finn's hands moving quickly over Ty's ass and legs. They swapped hot kisses in spite of the bad taste in their mouths.

"You saved my life," Finn said.

"You saved mine, too. He...it would have killed me after he'd finished with you."

Finn clung to him for a moment and Ty kissed his closed eyes.

"No more stinging?"

Finn shook his head, a small smile playing on his lips. He knelt at Ty's side and his mouth claimed Ty's cock.

"What are you doing?" Ty couldn't help grinning. He and Finn had worked up quite an appetite for one another. Washing off toxic sea sludge shouldn't have been a turn-on but oh, man, it was.

Finn's fingers stroked Ty's balls and ass. Ty moved his head out of the shower stream and took a deep breath, wondering if he'd remembered to lock the bathroom door. Who gave a fuck? Amadis could enter anyway, if he really wanted. He heard a voice outside the door but he was too far gone, desire exploding in his belly as Finn's incessant fingers began stroking his asshole.

"God...Finn," he belted out as a finger entered his ass. Finn's mouth tightened around Ty's cock. Ty humped the other man's face. Finn gave the best head Ty had ever experienced and there was *nothing* like an early morning blowjob in the shower. The combination of warm water and a hot, horny man with a talented tongue sent him into a wonderful orbit. He felt the pressure building in the base of his spine, and rose to his toes as if to brace himself for what would come next. He came so hard he almost fell over, grabbing the walls of the shower for support.

"I'm glad he didn't hurt anything important," Finn said when he finally released Ty's cock. He began to laugh as water ran down his face. "I just had to make sure."

Dizzy now, Ty turned off the taps. Damn the state's water shortage, that was one beautiful way to get over a near-death early morning experience.

The two men towelled off and brushed their teeth, walking into the hallway with towels wrapped around their waists. The house was filled with people.

Ty watched Finn turn the corner into his guest room in an unobtrusive way. He couldn't go into his room since it had now been cordoned off, but Amadis handed him some fresh clothes.

"Get dressed," he snapped. Geez, the guy was wearing his cranky pants this morning.

Back in the bathroom, Ty threw everything on and swiped deodorant under his arms a second time. He felt hot and sweaty already. Somebody from the Fire House must be here. He couldn't imagine why another elemental force would be here but then he heard a knock at the door and somebody calling his name.

Phillip Sedgwick. Surprised and delighted, he opened the door and hugged him. He looked sleep-deprived.

"Daine's here, in the kitchen with Chris. We need to talk."

"But Finn —"

"Finn is in good hands. Judge Paradis is here and he wants a word with you."

"He's here? In my house?"

Phillip nodded. "Houston, we've got a problem."

In the living room, Ty found himself surrounded by some of the elemental superpowers heaviest hitters. He was not particularly surprised to see Judge Fathom since he was the jurist in charge of the Kennedy trial. He was surprised to see Ephyrus Bainbridge and the other three partners leading the respective departments of the Elemental Superpowers most important law firm—Arden, the Fire attorney, Chinook, the Air representative and the Earth counsel, Damek.

Amadis stood next to Damek, arms folded across his chest, a homicidal look in his eyes.

"Good morning, Mr. Anglin," Bainbridge said, his tone clipped. "Care to explain how a certified sea monster wound up inside your home and attempted to kill the man entrusted to your safety?"

"I have no idea, sir."

"Is it true you were naked in bed together?"

Aw, shit. "Yes, sir. I won't deny it." He saw Amadis grin.

"Ordinarily, I would demand your immediate suspension with a full enquiry, but had you not been with him, Mr. Garrison would most certainly be dead."

"Yes, he would."

"You have any theories?" Judge Paradis asked him.

The full force of the combined Elemental Superpowers representatives made Ty break out in a sweat.

"Get him some water," Judge Fathom boomed.

Chris ran in with a glass of water and clasped his arm. "Finn's doing great. He's more worried about you," he said in low tones, though clearly everybody could hear him.

Marcel Paradis tried to keep a stern look on his face but was clearly passionate about his lover, Chris. The searing glance they exchanged left damp patches under Ty's armpits. Amadis rolled his eyes. For the first time since the man had walked in here, Ty took a long look at him. Dressed in faded denim jeans, a long white cheesecloth shirt topped with a long black leather coat and knee-high leather boots, Amadis was a fearsome sight. At six-foot, seven inches, he was too tall for any room, and his boyish features, long, white-blond hair and pale blue eyes gave him an angelic appearance. And he was...sort of. He was a water sprite.

There had been a time when Ty had been obsessed with him...and the feeling had been mutual. But Amadis, who was, by the oath of his court, to *love everybody*, took those words too far. He couldn't stay faithful if his dick depended on it. Or his life. There had been a time when Ty thought he would die without him. Now he only longed to be near Finn again.

Careful, guy. They might take him away from you, yet.

"We think there was outside interference," Bainbridge began.

"Really?" Ty couldn't keep the sarcasm out of his tone. "Look, I'm sorry if I sound frustrated but I am. I'm a good Water Marshal. I've never lost a client yet but this poor man has had three significant attempts on his life, twice right in front of me." He held up his hand as the chorus of voices tried to disrupt him. "And the second time, let's not forget, the attempt happened in a protected sanctum. Any clues how the invaders got into the Water Court?"

The silence that greeted his last words told him everything he needed to know. They were still no closer to getting any answers.

"There are three things to be considered," he said. A few of the men present started to speak, but he was pleased when Amadis spoke over them all.

"Let him talk."

Judge Fathom looked incredulous that an uppity water sprite would talk him down but he, too, remained silent.

"Firstly, they keep coming after Finn Garrison. Why?" Ty asked.

"Very good question," Bainbridge said. "There are other jurors on the panel."

"Exactly." Ty held up a finger. "The other jurors no doubt have protection now." He glanced at Amadis, who nodded. "But, still they come after Finn because, I suspect…and here we come to the second point…" He stepped forwards and as if moved by invisible ropes and pulleys, the others stepped forwards too, leaning towards him.

"I suspect, being a Water Mage, he is the most powerful man left on the jury and I bet, I'll just *bet*, they think that without a man of such morals and innate gifts, they're on the road to a not guilty verdict."

"The thought had crossed my mind," Judge Fathom said, "but it still doesn't explain how the culprit, or culprits, entered my courtroom with all its protections, or your own home, Tyros."

"This brings me to my third point. There's a serious violation of Elemental Superpowers Law here and it's bigger than fat boy Kennedy and his sleazy seaside royal family. I think this is the work of a freshwater entity trying to discredit all of us."

Fathom looked shocked. "Have you any basis for this…accusation?"

"I am merely putting forth suggestions. Let's look at some of our recent freshwater convictions. Anyone put away claiming innocence? Any cases that looked just a little bit dodgy? Kennedy's attorney claims his client has been framed. If that's the case, and I'm not saying it is, then this conspiracy is even bigger than we think."

"A freshwater conviction?" Judge Fathom seemed to ponder the point. "I should be offended, because I've never punished an innocent man yet, but…" His voice faltered and he glanced at Judge Paradis.

"I called Judge Fathom as soon as I heard what happened here," Marcel said. "I told him I thought this could have something to do with the Merrow twins."

"The Merrows? But they're in Wales…aren't they? And they're not freshwater people." Bainbridge looked confused.

"Some of them are. Some of them are here in the US. Two of the females married humans."

"Yes, but that case can't have anything to do with this."

"Who are the Merrows?" Ty asked, trying to follow the conversation.

"Not who, but what." Marcel's tone was grim. "The Merrows are Welsh water spirits. Mostly female… This was a sad story and an example of small town mania run amok."

"Let's not start that again," Bainbridge said.

"Why not?" Phillip asked. "Ty just said we should consider any recent verdicts and —"

"It's ridiculous," Chinook said. "All supposition."

"We have to start somewhere," Marcel insisted. "Remember, this case was about a male Merrow convicted of homicide. Males, as you know, are very rare in the species and his wife and twin sister have said for over a year now that he is innocent."

"Every convicted man claims innocence," Bainbridge said.

"This was different. And let's not forget…" Marcel cast a glance at Ty but bit off the rest of his statement. He paused. "Let's not forget there is a connection. The Appeals Court."

"I'm unfamiliar with that side of the case," Bainbridge said. "The appeals process is highly secretive. I'd have to launch an executive order for the results."

"I'll get you one," Judge Fathom said. "I'll also talk to the presiding judge. It was a most unusual case, I recall."

Ty's thoughts raced. He recalled the case vaguely, but had no idea if it was relevant.

"You mean the merman case?" he finally asked.

"That's the one." Marcel nodded vigorously.

"But…but…I remember that case. I thought there was no evidence and besides, I always thought they were gentle folk." His head was beginning to hurt.

"They are. Precisely. I wasn't part of the court system at the time but I did follow the case with some interest," Marcel said. "The judge had difficulties with this one."

"Yes, I remember." Judge Fathom seemed lost in thought. "I wonder…"

"Can somebody look into it?" Ty asked.

A few of the men stared at him.

"Of course," Judge Fathom said. "In the meantime, how do we keep our juror safe?"

"I'll take him to a safe house. There's a hole in our network somewhere," Ty said. "I propose that I take Finn to a place only known to Amadis and to Judge Fathom. Both are bound by secrecy and there can be no mistakes. No overheard conversations."

"Agreed," Judge Fathom said. He gave a wave of his hand. "I'd like everybody to leave us now. Not you,

Amadis. You stay right there. Tyros, please fetch your charge."

Just as Finn was starting to feel good from the yummy creations Chris and Daine kept plying him with, Ty came to the kitchen and took him into the living room.

"But I haven't finished my chocolate crème brulee," he whined. "Three bites left, Ty."

"I'll give you all the crème you can handle. Come on, sweetheart. We have to talk to the judge."

There was an odd feeling in the living room that Finn couldn't explain. It was as if the entire room couldn't decide if it was warm or cold, dark or light…it felt really weird.

"Finn," Ty began once they were seated at the dining table with Amadis and Judge Fathom. Judge Fathom was okay. Finn quite liked the old codger. Amadis was something else. He was a scary looking guy. Tall and slim, he had a muscular strength to him not immediately noticeable in his Bohemian clothing. He also had a cold fish look to his eyes that Finn found unattractive yet oddly compelling. He was certain something had happened romantically between Amadis and Ty but he tried not to feel jealous. Whatever it was must have happened a while ago and Ty's focus seemed entirely on Finn.

They all stared at him but he felt safe with Ty beside him.

"Where do you propose to take him?" Amadis asked.

"Finn, where do you feel safest?" Ty asked him.

"With you."

"Yes, that's lovely." There was a hint of desperation to Ty's tone. "But where in the world do you feel safest?"

"Oh, that's easy. In Bermuda."

"Bermuda?"

He could see the dismay on Ty's face and sought a way to retract his statement. "But of course, I'm quite safe—"

"You live in St. George's Town, don't you?" Judge Fathom asked.

Finn couldn't keep the smile from his face. "Yes, sir, I do."

"I so envy you," the judge said. His face took on a far-away expression. "I dream of those pink sand beaches, sitting for hours at the pub... Tell me, what is the population of St. George's these days?"

"About eighteen hundred people, sir."

"And there are very few cars...no freeways, no two-hour commutes?"

The idea of a freeway in his beloved Bermuda must have registered on his face because Ty grinned.

"How about crime?" he asked.

"Pretty low."

"The perfect hideaway, don't you think?" Judge Fathom looked at Ty for confirmation.

Ty shrugged. "I guess. But I don't know the island at all."

"I do. I can show you around," Finn said, pleased to see the spark of interest in Ty's big hazel eyes. And the tour would start with Finn's bedroom.

"Excellent," Judge Fathom said. "Amadis, I'll leave you to arrange the travel plans and—" He stroked his chin. "I think I'll plant the idea that you've gone to Big Sur. It's close and yet remote enough that it would be difficult to pin you down. I trust that none of you will discuss this conversation with anybody, including family members."

The three men gazed at each other.

"You will stay in touch with Amadis," the judge told Ty. "He'll alert you as soon as court is back in session." He looked very old all of a sudden. "This is a bad business," he said, shaking his head. "I can't help feeling we're on the tip of a supernatural catastrophe."

He turned and walked right through the wall, leaving a pool of water on the floor. Finn had seen only one other man do a thing like that. His father. He felt a chill running through him. He hoped the judge was wrong.

"I'll organise your trip myself," Amadis told Ty and Finn, "so there can be no accusations of a leak in *my* department." He shot dark looks at them as he pulled a cell phone out of his pocket. "I suggest you two start packing. Keep it light. We don't want to attract attention. And don't make any calls."

"He's a barrel of laughs," Finn muttered as he crossed the hallway into the guestroom.

"Yeah, I'd forgotten he could be a bit of an ass."

"Has it been over long?"

Ty looked like he was going to deny anything had gone on between him and Amadis, but it was futile.

"A long time. A long, long time. A thousand years ago." Ty's hand found its way to Finn's cheek. "Get ready. I want you to myself."

It was hard to feel churlish when the man said things like that.

Ten minutes later, they were riding a commuter bus to San Francisco airport. "At least he could have driven us to the airport. This is the itinerary from hell," Ty griped. "Look at this. We fly to Los Angeles, from there we go to South Carolina with two stops along the way and then we travel from there to Bermuda." He frowned. "It says we are not to travel by boat under any circumstances."

"That sort of makes sense because we're water people...and you know...if anyone catches wind of us heading back that way..." Finn was having the time of his life. He knew with absolute intuitive certainty that Amadis couldn't stand that Ty's affections were now elsewhere. Ty was oblivious to how pissed his former lover was.

"Yeah, but I'm starting to feel landlocked already." Ty leaned his head back against his seat.

"Just think about the pink sandy beaches and the low crime level," Finn said, keeping his voice down. "We'll be there before you know it."

The odd thing was the farther they got away from the neighbourhood, the more anxious he became. He adored Bermuda but what if he was tracked down there? What if the assassins came after him and Ty and they had no back up?

Now he was thinking clearly, he realised they'd been lucky that Amadis had turned up and the full force of the superpowers court system had supported them. He'd been adrift and alone, admittedly by choice, in Bermuda. But now, Ty was with him and it would be just the two of them. And his dotty father. How the hell did he explain the old man to Ty?

He wondered how and when to start but Ty seemed to be asleep. There would be time to explain the old man. He hoped. He wondered if he could even explain how supernatural brilliance had eventually pickled his dad's formidable brain. Finn worried about the same thing happening to him. Maybe they wouldn't even need to see the old guy. He'd acted befuddled when Finn had last gone to visit him in his home in Hamilton, the capital city of Bermuda. His father had asked him to repeat everything three times.

The worst of it was that his father had once been the most incredible water jurist in the supernatural world.

That was, until the strange case of the Merrows. His father hadn't been the judge on the case, but he had been one of the three Circuit Court of Appeals judges. Finn sighed. His father had been outvoted. He'd believed the Merrows had been innocent…then he lost his mind. The other judges easily convinced the High Court that Vincent Garrison had lost his marbles and his opinion on the Merrow case had no validity.

Or, Finn wondered now, did it?

* * * *

He found himself being shaken vigorously awake and panicked for a moment. Nothing was sitting on his face, but it was still an unpleasant sensation.

"Finn, sweetheart, wake up."

"Are we there yet?" He was so disoriented he couldn't see straight. They'd travelled for eighteen hours now and it had been a nightmare. Cancelled and delayed flights, an emergency landing in Charleston, North Carolina, a bizarre re-routing to Atlanta. Now they were at JFK Airport, waiting for their final Delta flight to Bermuda. At two hours and twenty minutes, it was a short flight, for which Finn was grateful. He checked the time on Ty's iPad sitting on his lap. It was six o'clock in the morning and the windows revealed a pearly sky swirling into sunrise.

"What's the matter?" he asked. Ty was staring at him.

"Your father was on the Appeals Court for a homicidal merman case."

"Yes, I know."

"How did he vote? The appeals docket is locked."

"He voted in favour of the defendant. He believed he was innocent."

Ty's eyes widened. "So, Marcel might have been right, except...if your father voted in his favour...I don't see why you're a target."

"What are you talking about?" Coffee. Finn needed coffee. "I'm going to grab a coffee. I see that cart over there opening up. Do you want one?"

"Yes, please." Ty bent his head over his iPad, pecking out keys with his index finger.

Finn felt a long-buried rage swelling in him as he approached the cart and waited in line. His poor father had stood by his decision — to his professional detriment, and perhaps even that of his sanity — in the Merrow case. He tried, as always, to look for the positive in any situation. Ah, yes. He loved the smell of fresh coffee. Everywhere around him on the concourse was evidence of their presence in an international airport. The food stalls boasted specialities from all over the country.

He ordered their coffees, and his gaze fell on some pecan praline cinnamon rolls. They wouldn't be as good as Christopher's cuisine, but they would do. They hadn't eaten all night, since the airport's stalls had all been closed. The vendors were starting to come to life but he didn't want to wait for something more substantial. He ordered four rolls and took his bounty back to Ty.

"Wonderful," Ty said, grabbing the coffee cups so Finn could settle in his seat again. "So, tell me about the Merrow case."

"It was horrible." Finn sighed. "It happened in Wales. Do you know much about the Merrows?"

"Vaguely." Ty sipped his coffee and moaned in appreciation when he opened the box of breakfast rolls. "These look so damned good."

"It happened a couple of years ago. A woman was driving home along a stretch of road. She apparently was on her cell phone and told her husband she saw a man in the sea waving to her. She thought he was seeking help. She was, by all accounts, a strong swimmer. She pulled over and ran to the water. Her husband tried to tell her to stop, but she dropped her phone on the sand and went in after the stranger.

"There were no witnesses except for the man's testimony of what he heard on the phone. He said he heard a man singing and his wife screaming, and by the time the police got there, she had drowned. She was floating face down in the ocean, a strange scaly piece of skin in one of her hands.

"Of course, the human forensic community couldn't identify it and said it was some extinct species of fish, but the supernatural community knew it was a Merrow—or, as you know, merman. Only one merman was known to reside in that area and he had married a human woman. Many Merrow do this. They produce offspring that can live on the land for years, but their curse—or gift, depending on how you view it—is that they must, at some point, return to the sea."

"And he did?"

"Yes. Andrew was his name. I don't remember the whole thing, except that my father said at the time that Andrew went back and forth between land and sea. Part of the reason my father didn't believe Andrew was guilty was because mermen are usually protectors of their particular stretch of water. If anything, my father was convinced that Andrew tried to save her."

Ty stared at him a moment. "So he was convicted?"

Before Finn could respond, the ground attendant announced that their flight was about to begin boarding. They had plastic cards in their possession putting them at the front of the line. They gathered their things and moved towards the boarding gate doors.

They didn't resume their discussion until they were seated side by side, upgraded to business class courtesy of the air crew, demolishing the last of their pecan rolls. The flight was only three-quarters full, giving a merry tone to the cabin. People were able to stretch out and happily did so.

"So, this...Andrew was convicted of homicide and he appealed," Ty said.

"Yes, my father is one of the senior judges in the Appeals Court. I never knew for years what he did. He poses as a simple fisherman in Bermuda."

"He does?" Ty seemed surprised.

"We're a very small community and he's always been the man people go to for advice, but he can hardly advertise his true calling. I began to suspect something was wrong when he would go out all day to fish and come home empty-handed. I thought he was seeing another woman, but it turned out he was doing official business. He's a Water Mage of the first order."

He wondered how much more he should tell Ty, but Ty was now fiddling with the in-flight magazine looking for music and movie channels.

"Oh, they give us food for free on international flights, I forgot," Ty said, sounding excited.

"There are some things I should explain about my father," Finn said.

"Oh, he sounds marvellous. Can't wait to meet him." Ty stuck his iPad ear buds into the arm rest and leant back, closing his eyes, a smile on his face. "Do me a favour, sweetheart. Wake me when they swing by with food."

Finn watched him for a moment. He should really tell Ty now. Better to let the truth out than wait until the horrible chance they'd run into his father. His thoughts stopped running rampant. The chances were his father would have no idea he was back on the island. There was no need to let him know immediately. He could wait a few days...or weeks...then call him and check up on him. He'd visit his father alone. No need to subject the man to public scrutiny. Even if it was Ty.

Finn nudged Ty awake. The other man removed an ear bud from his ear.

"Do I smell coffee?" he asked.

The attractive flight attendant smiled at them. "Good morning, gentlemen. I'm happy to tell you we'll be serving a full breakfast this morning. I can offer you pancakes and scrambled eggs or eggs Benedict. Which would you prefer?"

They both went for the eggs Benedict with side orders of bacon.

"This is the life," Ty said. "I could get used to this. Beats Motel Sixes and breakfast in roadside drives. You want a mimosa, sweetheart?"

Finn laughed. He was glad Ty was as much of a foodie as he was. He agreed to a mimosa. After all, he had nothing to do but relax once they reached Bermuda. The thought pleased him and kept him buoyed. He was in a pretty good mood all the way to the island. They landed, went through customs and exited to the main terminal in Hamilton. Finn's good mood evaporated.

There waiting for him, shouting and waving, was his father.

Holy shit.

"Wha...?" Ty's jaw dropped open. "Is that a grey wet suit?" he asked.

"Yes." Finn's spirits sank to his shoes.

Ty's eyes narrowed and his tone turned even more incredulous.

"Is that a fin I see in the back of it?"

"Just a small one," Finn said, defensively. *Shit, shit and double fuck. Why did this have to happen?* "I should have said something earlier, but I didn't think it would come up."

They strode towards his father who was now waving both arms in glee.

"My father thinks he's a shark."

Chapter Seven

If Ty thought this was strange, he didn't show it. He grabbed Vincent Garrison's hand and shook it with great enthusiasm.

"Good morning, sir. How nice to meet you. Finn speaks so highly of you." The two men shook hands.

Finn's father stood out in his grey shark suit, ankle socks and Birkenstocks, looking as crazy as ever. A few people pointed and stared, but there was something about his father that made people keep their distance.

He was the only man in long pants of any kind waiting to greet new arrivals. Every other man wore Bermuda shorts. It was something of a joke on the island, but still the fashion persisted, even for formal wear. It was perfectly permissible to wear good quality black Bermuda shorts with knee-length black socks and good shoes to a formal event.

Finn had never quite become used to the fashion and wore jeans as often as the weather permitted. He frowned at a woman taking his father's picture with her cell phone. A few kids giggled, but nobody approached them.

"Splendid!" his father boomed. "My old friend, Favian Fathom called me and told me to expect you." He grabbed Finn and clutched him to his chest. "I was a little hurt you hadn't called me yourself, but he explained that he told you not to contact anyone."

His father held him at arm's length. "You're looking good, my boy, very good, in spite of the attempts on your life." He kept an arm around him and returned his beaming smile to Ty. "And I believe I have you to thank for saving my son's life."

"It was nothing," Ty said, flushing a deep red. Finn was surprised his lover seemed in awe of his father. "I would gladly do it again." The gaze he sent Finn made Finn's toes wobble in his shoes. Ty knew his dad was completely crackers but still seemed to like him! Maybe insanity ran in his family, too?

"The car's out front." Vincent Garrison gestured. "Come on, we'll get you home and settled. I want you to stay with me."

"With you?" Finn began, "but—"

"No buts, son. I promised Favian I would vouch for your safekeeping. He tells me he thinks this might have something to do with the Merrow case. I don't see how, but come on, we'll talk about this over lunch."

"I love your car," Ty said as they stepped outside and into the snazzy black convertible Saab.

"Only residents are allowed to own and operate vehicles, and even then it's one car per family," Finn told him.

"What do you drive?"

Finn smiled. "I have four different scooters and I like to walk." He sat back as his father took off like a crazed fool. His driving had always been terrifying, but now that he'd taken to wearing his shark-fin suit, it was worse. He drove hunched over the wheel like a big grey dog about to poop.

Vincent negotiated the streets of the British colonial island with a breathtaking fearlessness that always surprised Finn. His father lived in a sprawling beachside ranch-style house on a private bay in Pembroke. Finn's mother, who had died five years before, had decorated the house in a comfortable, beach-bar style and his father had never deviated from her ways. Every last throw cushion and seashell she had put in the house was still there.

His father roared into the driveway and into the open garage. A flock of nesting Bermuda Petrels had taken up residence on a high beam in the garage. Ty stood from the car, looking transfixed as Vincent made little bird noises to the endangered birds.

"I came here when Dad first found them and the Audubon Society told us how to care for them," Finn told him. "We had to put on oven mitts and fix a special box with ribbons and rope, we put some straw in there, and they've done very well, haven't they, Dad?"

"Splendid." His father grinned. "Come inside, I'd rather not talk out here."

Inside the house, his father turned to them as he left his Birkenstocks in the hallway against the wall. His mother had disliked shoes on the hardwood floors and Finn followed suit. He was pleased to see Ty lining up his shoes beside his.

"Now, son, let me ask you, will our guest be needing his own bedroom or will he be bunking with you?"

Finn felt his cheeks burning.

"Just as I thought. I must say, I am pleased. Your taste in men is improving."

Ty laughed.

"Why don't you take a quick shower and we'll talk," his father suggested, "or would you prefer a swim?"

"A swim," both men said at once.

In his bedroom that his mother had kept as a mini Finn shrine—and his father was wont to do the same—Finn closed the door as Ty ran gleefully from one wall of trophies to another.

"I heard you dive for shipwrecks and found so many treasures," he said. "These photos are amazing."

"Most of the things I've found are in the Bermuda Maritime Museum," Finn told him. "I've found some amazing items."

"I'd like to see them. Will you take me there?"

Finn was taken aback. "Sure. If you want me to."

Ty turned to him. "Of course I want you to take me. I want to learn everything I can about you." He glanced at the bedroom door. "I am so pleased we get to share, but I really didn't think your father meant bunking when he said it."

"Oh, yes he did." Finn gestured at the bunk beds that had been in his room since he was eleven years old. He wished his mother hadn't kept his old Spiderman bedding. It was embarrassing.

"I hope we're going to be sharing one." Ty dropped a swift kiss on his lips. "I'm so excited to go swimming and then talk to your father."

Finn watched the man drop his pants and licked his lips. He really wanted to get his mouth and hands on that delicious cock again.

"We have time," Ty said. "And believe me, if we're bunking together, I'm going to demand my sexual rations."

Finn gave him another kiss. "Come on, get ready. I want to feel that water. They say Bermuda has the best, most healing waters in the world."

Whoever *they* were, they were right. Everything about Bermuda made people feel good and live longer. He thought gloomily of his mother's battle with lung cancer. It had shocked them all since she'd given up smoking many years before. She'd fought a courageous battle but he had seen his father draw into himself after her passing. He had thrown himself into cases to stave off depression. Now he concerned himself with his thoughts of being a shark.

"Thank you for being kind to my father," he said, as he stripped off and slipped on a pair of board shorts.

"He's wonderful." Ty squeezed his shoulder. They left the room, walked down the hallway where the call of the wild surf greeted them from the open back door.

"The sand really is pink!" Ty ran across it, squelching his toes in the ultra-fine grains. "And so soft, too."

Finn's father was already on the sand, peeling off his socks.

"Ah, there you are." He beamed at them. "I might catch us some lunch whilst we swim."

Oh, God. Ty thought his father was wonderful. Wait until he saw the old man catching a fish. He wanted to say something but didn't. It would hurt his father's feelings tremendously if he dared suggest he use a fishing line. He merely smiled and wished him happy hunting.

"Cod, I think," his father announced then did a great big belly flop close to shore. It looked like it should have hurt but he knew the old man enjoyed making a splash. Literally. He and Ty stepped into the breach as his father swam like a shark in circles, his fin bobbing and weaving across the waves as he moved farther out to sea. Cod was supposed to be rare most times of the year in Bermuda, but not to Vincent Garrison. He always caught the fish of his choice.

"It feels so good," Ty said when he came up for air. They frolicked in the water, chasing and splashing one another. Ty dived down and came back up with a piece of pink coral. The water was so clean and so clear, they could see his father's feet beneath the ocean's surface. Finn spotted a sea horse dancing close.

He pointed out the little creature to Ty, who swam to it. The two men chased each other a little more after the sea creature swam away, until they heard a shout.

They came up for air just in time to see Vincent Garrison striding out of the ocean in his shark suit, a flapping giant codfish struggling in his clenched jaws. He raised his fists in victory.

"Nice one, Dad." Finn cringed as he said the words.

Ty grinned. "That's awesome! Bet he's a superb cook." He waded back to shore, leaving a surprised Finn staring after him.

* * * *

Vincent Garrison made a fantastic lunch of codfish and roasted potatoes, which, Ty was happy to learn, was a traditional Bermuda meal. They also enjoyed a crisp green salad with lettuce from Mr. Garrison's garden and sliced fig bananas, another Bermuda speciality. Perhaps his favourite part of the meal was the wonderful alcoholic drink called a Dark and Stormy, which he learned was a mixture of Gosling's Black Seal Rum and Bermuda ginger beer. Ty enjoyed two drinks before he realised Finn was very quiet, picking at his lunch as Ty and Mr. Garrison, who insisted he call him Vincent, discussed the Merrow case.

"I had no idea you existed," Ty told the old man. "When I found out I was going to take care of Finn, my assistant, Becca, researched him. Nothing came up on you at all, until Mr. Bainbridge forwarded me your file."

Vincent beamed. He did that a lot. His smile made Ty smile and Finn increasingly more quiet. He'd have to tell the man that Vincent Garrison might have some self-identity issues, but there was nothing wrong with his mind. Ty should also tell Finn that he'd had a great-grandmother who thought she was a milk jug when she was alive.

"Well, you know they protect the identity of court judges until there is an actual case," Vincent said, "and I've been pretty much retired these last few years."

"But you work for the Appeals Court," Ty said.

"True, but there's not much call for appeals in the Water House. Earth and Fire on the other hand, their members are simply *prone* to violence. They have twenty-two Appeals Courts each. The Water House has five." He paused, biting into a potato.

"That business of drumming up charges against Daine Paradis for abuse of supernatural powers was just shameful." He slammed his hand on the dining table and several dishes jumped. "*Shameful!*" He swallowed his food, waving his fork around. "I mean, why didn't they come right out and tell Marcel Paradis they wanted him back on the bench?"

"Well, it all worked out in the end," Finn interjected. "Maybe he wouldn't have responded if they'd just contacted him."

"What a load of crap," Vincent said. "You want another Dark and Stormy, either of you?"

Finn and Ty nodded and the old man walked off to the kitchen.

"He's fabulous," Ty said. He could hardly breathe, he was so excited. He longed to ask the judge more questions. From what he'd read in the old man's files, Vincent Garrison had adjudicated many cases involving pirates and his very first trial had been as a juror at the age of eighteen in 1957 on the Boysie Singh case. One of the last known infamous buccaneers, Singh had been executed for the murder of his niece. What intrigued Ty was that it had been a human trial and he wondered what had happened that had led Vincent to the supernatural realm. He was also keen to hear his impressions of the legendary and scandalous Boysie Singh.

On the back deck with another drink, they lounged in comfortable chairs after lunch and he peppered Vincent with questions as Finn snoozed in the sun, a giant hat covering his face.

Vincent answered all of his questions, apparently delighted to have such a willing audience.

"What did you think of Boysie Singh?" Ty asked. "I've read so much about him. He sounds both fascinating and cruel."

"Very true. He was both. I mean, he was a hard man and certainly made no bones about his life as a pirate. He did some terrible things—smuggling drugs, people, murdering people—but he was also very interesting. Completely uneducated and yet quite well informed."

"He was hanged, wasn't he?" Ty noticed Finn removing the hat covering his face to watch his father as he spoke.

"Yes, and I went to his execution in Port of Spain. I felt if I could sentence a man to death then I needed to be man enough to witness his passing. It was not an experience I care to repeat."

"You haven't been to another execution since?"

"No, I have not." The now-subdued Vincent sipped his drink and gazed out to sea. Now maybe he was getting somewhere. Maybe the old man didn't really think Andrew the Merrow was innocent, maybe he just didn't like murder convictions.

"I know what you're thinking," Vincent suddenly said. "My son might not have told you, but I'm quite psychic, you know. We both are. Comes from my mother's side of the family. It's a bloody curse, if you want to know. My wife could never lie to me about her new dresses being old...or how much money she spent on shoes."

His face twisted in grief. "I'd give anything for one more day with her. I'd let her spend all the money she wanted on shoes. Even the ugly ones." He blew out a sigh. "I can tell you're thinking my queasiness about the execution is the reason I voted for the defendant in the case of Andrew Merrow."

"Well," Ty said, caught off guard, "frankly, the thought did cross my mind. Yes."

Vincent shook his head. "No. Nothing like it. I knew merfolk and they don't go around murdering humans. Humans lose their heads over merfolk, but more often than not it's the merfolk who get hurt. Their human spouses can't handle the fact that they never age and they also can't handle the realisation that as much as they love their partners, merfolk are more closely entwined with the sea."

"You seem to know a lot about them." Ty couldn't help feeling slightly suspicious despite the man's assurances.

"I studied them and I love them. I, as a shark, would never eat one of them. I have too much respect for their beauty." Vincent punctuated his statements with a finger pointing straight at Ty.

"But you have no problem eating a codfish."

Vincent stared at him. "I respect the codfish but they're not particularly sexy. On the other hand, I have always wanted to try eating a turtle since my friends tell me they taste just like chicken, but I can't bring myself to do it. I think they are also amazing and sexy creatures."

"I'm going to take a nap," Finn said. He got up off the chaise he'd been lying on and went inside.

Vincent sighed. "You love him, don't you?" he asked Ty.

"I'm not sure yet. I think, though, I am seriously in like."

"Don't be ridiculous. Love is love. I'm going to go catch some dinner. Go nap with my beautiful, difficult son, and tell him it's Harbour Night this evening. I expect you both to be there."

"Harbour Night? Okay, sure. We'll be there." *Whatever the heck that is.*

Ty got up and went to the bedroom he was sharing with Finn. He liked the idea of napping with the guy. Well, being horizontal with him. Sleep didn't necessarily need to be involved. He was surprised to find that Finn wasn't in the room. He walked through the house and heard a sound out front. He opened the door and poked his head outside. Finn was on a ladder, hammering at something on the roof.

"Hey," Ty said, "What are you doing?"

"Fixing the roof. Dad always forgets and then he runs short of water."

"Excuse me?"

"All the roofs in Bermuda are specially designed to catch rainwater and collect it for each home's use."

"Really?"

Finn stopped belting away with the hammer. "Yes, really."

"That's pretty nifty."

"Yep. It is." *Smack. Slap. Hammer. Hammity-hammity.*

"Can I help?"

"Nope. Almost done." Finn gave it a couple more bashes and seemed satisfied with his work. "Just got to put the ladder away."

Ty followed him to the garage. "Really? I can think of some good uses for it. I think you might enjoy at least one of them."

Finn laid the ladder against the garage wall and stepped outside, a big grin on his face.

"Sounds a little too athletic for me, but I'm keen to explore other…options."

"Oh, good. Come on. I'll race you inside."

They ran into the house, Finn looking the happiest he'd been since they'd arrived in Hamilton.

Finn arrived first, Ty closing and locking the door behind them. They stood facing one another. He should have been attacking the sexy man in front of him. Instead Ty found himself picking a fight with him.

"You're ashamed of your father." It was a statement, not a question.

Finn's face seemed to lose its colour. "I'm worried about him."

"Why? He seems happy."

"I found this." Finn handed him a piece of cream-coloured parchment.

"What is it?"

"Read it. You'll see."

Ty opened the folded sheet. He blinked a couple of times and re-read the thing. *Holy cat.*

"Yeah." Finn took the page out of Ty's hands. "A competency hearing. It's the third one they've sent. You see now, don't you? They're going to strip him of all his powers and then he'll have nothing. He's a magnificent man and his world is diminishing."

"Does he act this way in open court?" Ty asked. He had to stop acting like it was all fine and wonderful that the great Vincent Garrison thought he was a shark.

"He hasn't...yet. But the word is out and now, of course, the Merrow case has opened things up again. They want to get rid of him, clearly in case there are more appeals in this case...or some other one."

"We're here now. His trial's in four days. No way the case back in California will be back on the dockets before then. We'll help him."

Finn's eyes moistened. "We?"

"Of course. Finn. I'm crazy about you and your old man. I don't care what he thinks he is, I happen to think he's amazing...and I actually don't think he really believes he's a shark. He's just a man trying to find a little bit of joy in his life."

"You think so?"

A stray tear ran down Finn's face. It almost broke Ty's heart. The man had been so stoic about everything that had happened to him, yet here he was—so emotional about his father. He would do everything in his power to help them both.

"I'm here for you," he said. "I'm a Water Marshal. I'm here to help."

Finn rushed into his arms, covering his face with kisses. Ty kissed him back, the fever raging between them. Ty tried to remember when they'd last made love. He recalled getting a damned fantastic blowjob in the shower from Finn the previous morning. Man, that seemed like a long time ago. He put his hands on Finn's face, gulping for air between kisses that didn't stop.

He felt Finn's cock hardening against his thigh. He was such a hot man. For a moment, Vincent's statement about water elements not being violent flashed through his mind. What he felt for Finn was pure, raging passion. He flung the man to the floor, unable to wait to get to the bottom bunk.

Ty hovered over Finn, whose arms wrapped around his neck. Their cocks collided in their respective shorts, rubbing against one another. It was an amazing feeling, transporting Ty back to his teenage years.

He peeled off the still damp board shorts from his lover's thighs, his tongue tracing a salty path along Finn's treasure trail. Finn was such a responsive lover. He began squirming right away as Ty delved into the crotch of the shorts to retrieve the thick, hard cock he had come to crave. The head leaked just a little, a mixture of salty sweetness as he licked and sucked on it. Finn's cock entered his mouth, and Ty felt Finn weave his hands in his hair, urging him to continue.

Finn struggled completely out of his shorts, shoving them aside.

"I need to taste you," he rasped.

Ty lifted his head as Finn reached for him. He allowed Finn to unsnap his shorts, pulling them down, his own hard cock bouncing right into Finn's waiting hands as Ty grinned and raised himself up to kiss Finn's waiting mouth. Their kisses became urgent as Ty felt Finn encircling his cock with his hand, holding it against his own—slowly, gently, jerking on their joined shafts.

God...he was great. Ty moved down, with Finn protesting as he was forced to release Ty from his trusty grip. He began sucking again, but Finn grumbled. "I still wanna taste you."

Ty flipped around so his cock was over Finn's face. Finn grabbed Ty's hips and began sucking his cock as Ty resumed his own taste test.

The thought occurred to him—Finn tasted better than blancmange.

He sucked and pulled, surprised when Finn's mouth released Ty with a loud pop. He began to roam Ty's ass with his tongue. Oh...God. Ty buried his face between Finn's ass cheeks and began licking, too.

The two men moaned, their cries muffled. It was a difficult position in which to mutually rim, but oh, so pleasurable. Ty fell to the side as Finn's tongue began stabbing at his hole. It was too much. He took his face from Finn for a moment to enjoy the sensation then reciprocated on Finn. The man's ass was a fine piece of art.

They sucked and licked one another, their tempo increasing. Finn's cock streaked hot juices across Ty's neck. He had to suck that cock. Ty moved back, recapturing the silken shaft just begging for his tongue.

Finn, too, began sucking and licking on Ty. The sensation of warm waves rolling within him was deep and beyond pleasurable. Ty clung to Finn's thighs to keep the man in his mouth as he began to come hard.

He felt Finn's fingers probing his ass. Ty scurried to stroke his lover, too.

They came together, a storm of hungry release — licking, tasting and taunting long after their shared eruption flamed out.

"I love that we couldn't wait to get to bed," Finn said, putting a hot kiss on Ty's ass.

Ty lifted his face from the other man's thigh.

"I don't think I ever wanted anyone this much, Finn."

Finn reached down and stroked his head. "And it's only going to get better."

* * * *

Vincent banged on the bedroom door some time later. How much later, Ty wasn't sure, but with Finn burrowed into Ty's body, their legs entangled, it wasn't a pleasant interruption. Ty slowly unwound himself from the other man.

"Dinner's up!" Vincent roared and Finn moaned as Ty moved away from him.

"His timing could improve," Finn said, sitting up and rubbing his eyes like a little kid. They grabbed clean towels then jumped into the shower across the hall. Afterwards, Finn lent Ty a pair of his Bermuda shorts from his substantial collection in his bedroom.

"Dress like the natives," Finn said, smiling. "Oh, I smell Cassava pie!" And he was off and running.

Ty followed him to the living room, where he found Vincent dressed like a shark. He caught Finn's flickering gaze, dismay etched in his lover's eyes, quickly replaced by a smile.

"You made it, Dad? How wonderful."

"Your mother's recipe." Vincent tapped the top of the massive pie with his steak knife. "I hope it tastes as good as it looks."

The men took their seats as the sun started to set outside the windows. Ty liked that the large windows were unadorned, looking straight onto the ocean. The horizon, rimmed in soft pink, looked almost like the opening of a clam shell — a breath-taking accompaniment to the pink sand just visible from where he stood.

Vincent began to slice the pie, which to Ty's astonishment, was a savoury creation in spite of having two pounds of sugar in it.

"Two pounds?" he bleated, as he bit into the wonderful, rich, thick goodness. "Oh, my God. What is in this?"

"Don't you think Daine and Christopher should make a Cassava pie cupcake?" Finn asked between bites and licking his fork.

"Absolutely."

Vincent seemed very happy that they liked his pie, which, he informed them, contained ten pounds of cassava root, which the first settlers from England grew and used in place of flour. It also contained eighteen eggs, an entire boiled chicken, two pounds of pork, nutmeg, mace and other spices.

Ty ate a second helping, washing it down with ice cold island beer. Then they were on their way to Harbour Night. They walked to Front Street, the main street in Hamilton — now blocked to all vehicular traffic. Bright, swinging lanterns graced the eaves of every store on the street which now operated as a kind of arts and crafts fair, from what Ty could tell. They went from store to store and stopped by all the booths.

A bouncy, inflatable slide and castle operated at one end with tiny tots bouncing and screaming inside it.

At well-lit booths, local artists plied their crafts — everything from jewellery to sand art. Ty felt the urge to buy. He was a terrible consumer. He could be persuaded to buy almost anything, but he resisted the temptation of even the tiny pictures of palm trees painted on pieces of driftwood. They had to travel light. They'd come all the way here from California with cabin baggage, and that's how they would go home.

A local band struck up *God Save the Queen* on a soundstage and everyone stood to silent attention. It was a stirring reminder that Bermuda was British ruled. The crowd applauded and the merry business of buying and selling continued. There was a charming, New England tone to the buildings. Ty envied Finn's youth here. It seemed a wonderful place to live.

Live. God...what about the future? What if we want to be together? Where would we live?

"The Gombey dancers are coming," Vincent shouted and they rushed to the edge of the street to watch the arrival of the colourfully clad dancers who performed to such happy reggae music, Ty felt like dancing.

And then his cell phone rang. It was Judge Fathom.

"Kennedy escaped custody," he said, when Ty was able to find a spot quiet enough to hear him. "We caught him again, but he had significant help in getting away from us. We've now put him into maximum security in an undisclosed location. I tell you, Tyros, this has been the most unpleasant case it's ever been my misfortune to handle."

The judge hung up on him before Ty could respond. What did this mean for the trial? Was it evidence of

Kennedy's guilt or innocence? And what did Fathom mean by 'significant help'?

"Everything okay?" Vincent asked him, touching his shoulder. Beside him, Finn looked grave. Ty repeated what the judge had told him.

"This is a bad business," Vincent said, shaking his head. "Very bad. And I've been thinking. I was hoping to take you to the Hog Penny for a beer, but maybe it's time we visited Andrew Merrow. Let's ask him what he knows about any of this."

Finn and Ty exchanged glances. "Isn't he in custody?" Ty asked.

"Most certainly he is, but he's a merman. He's in water. A secret body of water."

"Where?" Ty was afraid to ask.

"My back yard, of course."

* * * *

Ty had never met an actual merman, but grew up listening to stories of mermaids luring human men to their watery graves. He had known his family worked in the Water House. His grandfather and father had both been Water Marshals. He'd resisted following in their footsteps. He'd wanted to be a carpenter. His father had gone mad at the idea.

Jesus was a carpenter, he was fond of reminding his father, but he found that the pull of the supernatural world was hard to resist. When his grandfather died, Ty took it hard. He wished every single day that he'd asked him more questions because now he took great pride in his vocation, and the duties of a Water Marshal seriously. He felt he was still learning new things every day. He never stopped learning. His own father was rather taciturn and only gave advice or information in small increments. It was very frustrating.

They walked home, his hand brushing the back of Finn's hand in the encroaching darkness. Ty wondered how gay-friendly Bermuda was, but now was not the time to ask—or to take the man's hand into his—no matter how much he wanted to touch Finn. There would be plenty of time in bed later tonight.

At the house, they kicked off their shoes just inside the door, and Vincent led the way out back.

"He's been in your custody the whole time?" Ty asked, incredulous.

"Yes." Vincent nodded, his gaze on the now choppy ocean water.

He began singing in a strange, hypnotic way. The moment transfixed itself in Ty's mind as a milestone. He felt tears pricking the back of his eyes. He glanced at Finn, who also felt the strong emotion rolling between them, like a fine mist.

"Did you know Andrew was here?" he asked Finn.

Finn shook his head.

Vincent walked down to the water's edge. Finn covered his face with his hands, as if unable to believe what was happening.

"He's not crazy," he said. "My God! All this time I thought he was mad, and he's been doing this for Andrew—dressing like a shark to make the poor man feel safe!"

Vincent paced the ocean shore, talking in a strange language and singing louder now. The water rippled in little pools. Somebody or something was just under the surface.

"If that's the case, he needs to tell the committee," Ty said. "We'll tell them together."

"We can't," Finn said, tears streaming down his cheeks when he lifted his hands from his face. "He takes his guardianship of sea creatures seriously. What the hell are we going to do, Ty?"

Ty felt the tears, too. He brushed them away. Dammit. There was a way. He'd involve his father, and Judge Fathom, too. He'd explain. They'd have to understand.

"Oh, my God," Finn's tone sounded awed. "Have you ever seen anything so lovely?"

The night took on a silver hue as the most magnificent looking man Ty had ever seen rose to the surface. He'd seen that face in his dreams. The man smiled at them both, but his pure and total adoration was for Vincent, his protector.

"Vincent, how are you?" the merman asked, his voice sounding like a river flowing against rocks. It was a wonderful sound.

"My lovely friend, I am well. I am afraid we must ask you some questions. There have been three attempts on my son's life. Now, I know the women in your life are proud, determined and fully believe in your innocence, but is there any chance they had anything to do with this?"

Andrew looked aghast. Ty realised his handsome torso was the only part of him visible. As his eyes adjusted to the strange, supernatural light, he saw the rest of the merman and was surprised how long his tail was. It looked almost like a gigantic sea snake.

Vincent began speaking in the strange language he'd started using before and Andrew spoke in kind. He went from being angry to incredulous.

"Finn, son of Vincent," Andrew called out, his voice drawing Finn like an invisible thread towards him.

Ty accompanied him, afraid the merman would grab his lover.

"Finn, I assure you, I have had nothing to do with this. I have wallowed in despair, it is true, with only your father for company, but he has treated me with kindness and grace. My wife, my dear cherished wife, is human and lives in Wales. She has taken our children and left me. I can't imagine it's possible, but my sister, my lovely twin, did move to California recently. I stopped hearing from her, but if she has anything to do with this monstrous crime, I cannot support it."

"She moved to California?" Ty asked.

The merman stared at him, as if noticing him for the first time.

"Yes, Tyros, son of Tyros Senior."

"What does she do there? What is her name?" Finn asked.

"Her name is Magenta, but as to what she is doing there, I can't say."

Ty's brain snapped into auto focus. Magenta. Why was that name familiar? *Holy heck. Magenta!* He gazed at Finn, who stared back at him.

"It couldn't be, could it?" Finn asked, his voice low.

"What is it?" Andrew asked, his tone frightened.

"Magenta is working in the kitchens of Fabulous Cupcakes," Finn said.

"Helping my cousin, Easter Sunrise," Ty added.

His thoughts raced. *Magenta was there when they had talked about Ty taking Finn home with him. She knew! Could all this be circumstantial?*

He would have spoken again except that Andrew began to wail. The sound was heartbreaking. Listening to a merman cry was something Ty hoped never to experience again. The merman wept such heart-wrenching tears and swam away.

And then the skies opened up and it began to rain.

Chapter Eight

Fascinated by the sight of the merman vanishing back under the waves he had emerged from, Finn watched the silver hue Andrew had brought with him slowly dim in the falling rain. Tears running down his own face at the hopelessness of Andrew's and their situations, it took him a while to realise that something else was wrong.

The rain was strange. There was something dark and threatening about it, the water almost aggressive on his skin. He flinched as several large drops hit him in the face in rapid succession, almost as if a water gun had propelled them in his direction. The water felt...harsh.

"Well, this is weird." Finn's father frowned as he turned back from the open sea. All traces of pretending to be a shark were suddenly gone.

"You feel it too?" Finn held out his hands to capture some of the strangely large drops, brought a wet finger to his lips and tasted it. "Salty!"

"Salty rain? But that isn't possible." Ty's eyes widened and he repeated the test, sticking a wet finger into his mouth and making a production of licking it clean when he noticed Finn staring at him. Ty winked.

Finn grinned. His Water Marshal sure was one for only believing the evidence of his senses. But it was the naughtiness of his movements and his provocative gaze which made it all worth it. He could watch Ty go on like this forever. Well, that or until he came in his pants.

God, the man was distracting him again. They had a serious problem of supernatural proportions here, and he was letting his attention wander. He cleared his throat, forcing himself back on track.

"There is something seriously wrong here. Ty is right—rain cannot be salty. Well, not under normal circumstances." Finn's father turned back towards the house. "We need to get inside, and quickly."

They ran back to the house, raindrops of increasing size pelting them violently, making their progress difficult. The water hissed when it touched their skin now, almost burning Finn by the time they made it indoors. The rain bombarded the roof and came in through any available opening, causing little puffs of noxious smoke when it touched the carpet.

"Quick, close all the windows." Finn's father locked the door. "It looks like we're under attack and I'll need to execute a Wave Order to protect us and the house."

"Under attack? What the fuck? Who even knows we're here?" Ty frowned, but raced off to check upstairs.

Finn helped his father on the lower floor, worrying about the situation and slightly awed that his dad was going to attempt enclosing the whole house in the watery supernatural bubble. That would require a lot more power than most Water Mages had at their disposal. But then again, hadn't his father more than proven that he was anything but ordinary?

When they were done and Ty returned to the living room, Finn's father stood very still in its centre, closed his eyes and started humming.

"If that's a Wave Order…" Ty shook his head.

Finn's father continued humming for a good five minutes, Finn and Ty watching him raptly. All the colours of the rainbow started swirling about him, the very air becoming charged with electricity. No light came in from the outside, since it was fully dark by now, but the familiar feelings of euphoria told him when the protective bubble had completed.

His father looked a little pale and staggered to the sofa.

"Whoa." Finn was next to him in seconds, supporting his shaking body.

"What is going on?" Ty sat down at his side, eyes wide.

"It was a little harder than I thought to get the Wave Order up and running." Finn's father took a deep breath and relaxed against the sofa's back. "This attack isn't just strange, it's a lot more vicious than I expected."

"But who would be attacking us? And why? And what about that weird salty rain?" Ty raked his hair. "Or is this another attempt at Finn's life?"

"It could be." Finn's father grimaced. "Seems a little over the top for that, but it is possible. I thought you said only Judge Fathom and this Amadis person know where you are?"

"They are the only ones." Ty nodded. "And I don't think either of them would be willing, or capable, of organising something like this. I mean, what does it take to make rain salty?"

"An extremely powerful Water Mage could probably do it, but it is a corruption of every superpowers law there is. More than that, I think the rain was turning to acid just before we made it inside." Finn's father sighed. "A sure sign of pure evil."

"Acid rain exists?" Finn had a hard time stopping his jaw from dropping.

"Well, yes, and not in the way humans think about it." His father sat up, switching into teaching mode. "Before the four elemental superpowers were separated, each given their own laws to rule their use, the situation was a lot more chaotic than today. Different elements interfered with each other, creating chaos. The major threats of today are remnants of that. Just think of a tsunami as Water and Earth forces working together, or a major lightning storm where you have Air and Fire colliding."

"True." Finn nodded. Why had he never thought of that? Because he wasn't a philosopher, that was why. He was a practical Water Mage, not a theoretician.

"So acid rain is—what?" Finn still looked confused.

"Acid rain is a total perversion, because it requires the forces of Earth, in the form of minerals or volcanic ash, to work together with water. It isn't a natural link at all, at least not since the planet has cooled down and the elemental forces have separated into different domains." Finn's father rubbed his temples. "All of which goes to say that something like acid rain pelting us like it's doing now would take some major doing, and is in clear violation of all the laws we have."

"Which brings us back to the question of who is doing this." Ty looked thoughtful. "If we assume, which we have to for now, that this isn't directed against Finn or me, since the only people who know we're here are officers of the law of the highest order, we have to assume the attack is directed against you, Mr. Garrison."

"It's Vincent, and that makes sense." Finn's father smiled. "They must realise the outcome of the competency hearing they've been trying to drag me to is a little too iffy for their tastes."

"Who exactly are 'they', Dad?" Finn couldn't believe his father was so nonchalant about this. His reputation was about to be shredded, and Andrew's life might be in danger if his protector was suddenly taken away. Sure, the authorities would appoint a new jailer, but Finn doubted whoever it was would be so sympathetic to Andrew's plight. Not half as understanding, either.

"The same people who wanted Andrew put away despite the fact he was innocent, of course." His father looked decades older all of a sudden. "I didn't know all the details at the time of the trial—all I could see was a total lack of evidence for the merman's guilt. But Andrew has confided in me since then, so I know it was all an act of personal revenge."

"Revenge?" Finn's mouth dropped open. "For what?"

"I can't tell you any details without breaking his confidence—"

"I think you may have no choice." Ty had gone all Water Marshal, his back stiff and his face stern. "We are not only looking at a misdirection of justice, but at an attempt to disqualify you to ever use Water Power again. Not to mention they now seem to be ready to assassinate you as well."

"But I have no proof." Finn's father looked up.

"I can't believe I'm going to say this, but I don't care." Ty sighed. "Once I have reason to suspect foul play, I can get the case reopened. Then we'll be able to look for the proof officially."

"You're not going to believe this." Finn's father took a deep breath.

"Try me." Ty looked determined, leaning slightly forwards so he wouldn't miss a single word.

Finn pressed himself back into the sofa, feeling as if he was in the way, sitting between the two of them.

"The person who is behind this, according to Andrew, is..." Finn's father almost seemed to enjoy the rapt attention he was getting. "...Louis Hydros."

"What?" Ty jumped up, turning around to stare at Finn's father.

"Huh?" Finn was far less coherent. "Him again?"

"Why *again*?" Finn's father frowned. "What else has he done?"

"Well, we have as little proof as you do in Andrew's case, but it looks as if he might be one of the people framing Kennedy." Ty started pacing, mumbling to himself.

"Kennedy was framed?" Finn's father slumped back against the sofa's back. "I don't get it. First Andrew, now Kennedy? But it doesn't make sense."

"You've got it." Ty stopped pacing and stared at them. "None of this makes any sense at all. Add this confusion with the attempts on Finn's life—which may or may not be linked to the Kennedy trial—the mysterious involvement of Andrew's twin Magenta and her role in getting us into trouble, and you've got a supernatural mystery of epic proportions."

"Well, it's a good thing you're the Water Marshal in charge, then." Finn grinned at Ty's shocked expression. "What? I trust your abilities, sweetheart."

"I'm flattered, but this is all a bit much. I think I need help." Ty sank into one of the easy chairs and put his head in his hands.

"What about Julian?" Finn was sure Ty could do this on his own if need be, but finding out what the Water Detective had discovered while they'd flown across the country might be a good idea.

"Julian!" Ty looked up. "Of course, how could I forget?"

Ty was reaching for his phone when it started ringing.

Everyone jumped and Ty almost dropped the thing. He checked caller ID and his eyebrows rose.

"Guess who?" Ty opened the phone without waiting for an answer. "Julian, are you psychic?"

"Psychic? What are you talking about? Not last time I checked. Anyway..." Julian's voice shook. "I'm just calling to let you know we need you guys here. As soon as possible, if not before."

"Why? Have you found any evidence against Louis Hydros?" Ty had the distinct feeling that a dark vortex was about to suck him into its depths. There was a very weird vibe about this and he'd rarely felt so threatened in his life.

"Evidence against that super-criminal is the least of my worries right now, believe me. The shit is about to hit the fan, big time, and we'll need to stand together if we want to get out of this alive. And I'm not just talking Elementals either." Julian took a deep breath. "Judge Fathom and Ephyrus Bainbridge have been trying to avert disaster using the legal system, and I have supported them, but it doesn't look like we're getting anywhere. We need every Water Mage we can get if we want to save the city."

"What the hell is going on?" Ty sat up straight, really worried now.

Finn was as white as polar ice, and his father wasn't doing much better. The Wave Order's odd echo effect had ensured both men had heard every word of Julian's strangely worried speech.

"Just make sure you get here as soon as you can, both of you. And bring Finn's father as well! Sorry, gotta go." Julian ended the call.

"Shit." Ty closed his phone and leant back in his chair. "How are we going to get out of here while we're under attack? Never mind make our way all the way to San Francisco despite the fact we don't even have flight reservations."

"We're going to have to pool our resources." Finn frowned. "Getting away while we're under attack is going to take everything we have. But once we're out of here, I don't want us to use airplanes again. We'd need Amadis to help us, since he has all the information, and I'm still not sure we can trust him. He was giving me some pretty strange looks. And all those weird re-routings on our way here… If Julian is right about whatever catastrophe is threatening San Francisco, we'd better be there faster than eighteen hours from now. From the sound of it, it might all be over by then."

"I think Amadis is okay. He's an employee of the Water Court, after all. And anyway, what choice do we have? We're not Air People, so we can't exactly fly on our own. Water Power isn't suited for fast transportation. Then there is the matter of a whole continent between Bermuda and home." Ty sighed. Daine or Christopher might be able to help them, but they weren't here.

"I'm afraid I have to agree with Finn." Vincent leant forward in his chair. "We cannot trust anyone at this point. And the good news is we don't need anyone, since we have two Water Mages at our disposal."

"What does that have to do with anything?" Ty looked from Vincent to Finn, watching both of their grins grow. "What?"

"You said that Water Power isn't suited for fast transportation, and, under normal circumstances, you're right. But we're facing what looks like an extraordinary threat here, so we'll let you in on a little secret." Vincent stopped smiling. "But you have to promise on your honour as a Water Marshal, not to share this knowledge with anyone. Only Mages know, and we want to keep it that way."

"Okay, I promise." Ty nodded. Anything if it got them out of here quickly and safely. He had a very bad feeling about what was going on. He'd never seen Julian this upset and worried.

"Are you ready, son?" Vincent looked at Finn.

"I think so." Finn swallowed. "You do know that I've never done a Rapid before, right?"

"I didn't think you had. It's not exactly something we practice at Mage School. I'll take the lead, so you don't have to worry. As long as you know the procedure, remain focused on the target and are quick enough to transform the power from the collapsing Wave Order into the Rapid, we should be fine." Vincent raised his eyebrows. "Any other questions?"

Finn shook his head.

"Exactly how dangerous is this?" Ty had a funny feeling in his stomach. He had no idea what this type of Water Power involved, but the fact that Finn had never done it wasn't encouraging. What if the man got hurt? He'd never forgive himself.

"It's no more dangerous than the long distance transportation Fire People use. It's just less smooth and takes more energy." Vincent grinned. "Enjoy it while it lasts. Very few people inside the Water House have ever experienced this."

Why didn't that reassure him?

"So, where do we want to go?" Finn got up at the same time as Vincent and they stood close together.

"I'd suggest you join us, Ty." Vincent motioned him towards them.

Ty took the few steps necessary to stand next to them, more nervous than ever when Finn took his hand.

"The best place to aim for is somewhere on a beach." Vincent took Finn's then Ty's hand and closed the circle. "This could get wet."

"Wet?" Ty's confidence hadn't exactly been high to begin with, but now? What was he getting himself into?

"Yes, wet." Vincent grinned. "We *are* Water People, after all."

"I think my temporary home at the beach would work." Finn's hands squeezed Ty's in a gesture of comfort, or else it was nerves.

"Sounds good." Vincent nodded. "Okay, so you picture our destination, I'll execute the Rapid and Ty, you just…focus on our safety. And whatever you do — don't open your eyes before I tell you it's safe!"

Ty rolled his eyes but didn't say anything.

Vincent and Finn closed their eyes so Ty followed their example. At first, there was silence. After a while he thought he was able to hear the muted sounds of the acid rain hammering on the bubble of the Wave Order around the house. But he wasn't sure — it might just have been his imagination.

The soft hissing quickly rose to a crescendo of noise, sounding as if waves were crashing into the walls around them. Ty's feet got heavier and he felt water all around him. Right before he opened his mouth to ask what was going on, the water seemed to rise above his head. He held his breath and focused on remaining conscious as they started turning in circles.

Shit, this feels as if we're in some sort of vortex.

A pounding vibration went through them and something pushed them forwards, then sideways and backwards, as they rotated in the centre of their circle. They were swept up and Ty felt as if he was in a river rapid being carried to his destination with no influence on where he was going. Safety and keeping them together was the only thing on his mind as he gripped Finn's and Vincent's hands more tightly and hoped his oxygen wouldn't run out before they arrived.

Finn's warm hold on his hand was his only anchor as they were swept, who knew where, in a violent maelstrom of convincingly real-feeling water. It didn't last very long. With a huge crash, he landed on his butt on what felt like sand. Finn was on top of him and Vincent to his left. The water ran off them and left him dripping and shivering in a chilly wind.

He took a careful breath.

Everything seemed to be okay, but he wasn't going to risk it. Superpowers were no joke and when a Water Mage told you to wait for the all-clear before opening your eyes, he figured it was safer to do as he was told.

"Finn?" Ty longed to hear the other man's voice. It was nice to have him pressed up against his entire body, even if they were both fully dressed, but he needed to hear Finn's voice, wanted to see his lover.

"It's okay." Finn sounded out of breath, hugging him awkwardly with one arm while not letting go of his hand.

"Yes, we're fine." Vincent's voice from his left was steady. "We made it, and you can open your eyes."

Ty tore his eyes open. It was a good thing it was dusk or he'd been blinded. The rays of the day's last sunlight reflecting on the ocean's surface made him blink. He looked around. Finn's bungalow was behind them, Christopher and Marcel's house—all lit up and looking tempting, warm and welcoming—a bit farther along the beach.

Before he could say another word, the door of the house was opened and a worried-looking Marcel emerged.

"There you are! What took you so long?" The irate man marched towards them, waving his arms as if that would make him—or them—move faster. "Come on, we've got a catastrophe to avert. What are you waiting for?"

Finn pushed up and held out his hand to help pull up Vincent. Ty managed to get to his feet on his own, but he was still dizzy and dripping water all over the sand. His clothes were clinging to his shaking body and he felt as if he'd been on a white-water rafting trip gone wrong.

"Damn, this Rapid stuff is powerful." Ty grabbed his head as if that would make the swaying stop.

"Before we do anything else, we need a hot shower and some dry clothes, please." Finn grinned and took Ty's hand, lending silent support.

"The hot shower won't be a problem, and Christopher and I will make sure your clothes are dry by the time you're done. Just leave them outside."

Marcel turned towards Vincent and held out his hand. "Good to see you again, man."

"It's been too long." Vincent smiled and shook hands with Marcel as if they were old friends.

Heck, maybe they were?

"Indeed." Vincent and Marcel took the lead and started walking towards the house.

Ty and Finn followed, quietly holding hands. He was looking forward to a bit of alone time with Finn, even if it was only for the duration of a shower. Warm, wet time with his lover sounded a lot more fun than what they'd just been through.

* * * *

A hot shower and some very hot, gentle loving later, Finn emerged from the bathroom to find their clothes neatly folded on top of the bed in the guestroom. Now dry and nicely warm, he quickly slipped into them before Ty emerged from the bathroom. If he was still naked when his lover made it out here, there was no way they'd leave the room without making love.

Finn wished they had the time to do as they wanted. Instead, they had this catastrophe on their hands. It made him wonder if being a juror was worth it. Granted, none of his previous cases had been this chaotic, but one of these was enough for a lifetime. He didn't want to run the risk of facing something like this again. Discovering and salvaging lost shipwrecks or teaching swimming was a lot less stressful.

"Ready to go?" Ty was dressed and stood by the door.

How had that happened? Finn decided he was probably still exhausted from supporting his father in executing the Rapid. What a rush that had been! But he was bone-deep tired now. All he could do was hold on and hope they could avert whatever crisis was looming.

"Sure." Finn followed his lover and came to an abrupt stop when they entered the living room.

He'd expected Marcel and Christopher to be there, probably Julian, if he'd been given enough time to make it here. The number of people who were actually present stunned him.

Julian had made it and sat at one end of the sofa, next to Marcel. Christopher ran in from the kitchen, deposited a tray with hot snacks on the low coffee table then raced back mumbling something about sweet treats and drinks. Judge Fathom sat on Julian's other side, flanked by Amadis and Finn's father on chairs which had been brought in from the dining room. Mr. Bainbridge and Mr. Pontus sat in two of the easy chairs, joined by two strangers who had taken the remaining armchairs.

One looked like a fire-breathing hellion with silver hair and blue eyes, totally wrinkle-free despite the aura of age and experience he exuded. The other had an airy feel about him, with bluish skin and short, wind-blown white hair. He appeared almost insubstantial.

"Glad you could join us. Please have a seat." Judge Fathom pointed at two empty chairs that had been pulled up to complete the circle. "I think you know everyone here, except my esteemed colleagues, Judge Sexby, from the Fire Court, and Judge Nephelus, from the Air Court."

Finn sat down with an audible thunk. *What the hell is going on?*

Ty was still standing when Christopher bustled back into the room with a tray full of glasses and two big carafes of what looked like iced tea. Finn nudged his lover and he sat down while Christopher made sure everyone had a drink before he sat down next to Marcel.

"We are here to determine the best way to proceed in the case of Superpowers versus Louis Hydros." Judge Fathom took a sip of his iced tea, nodding in approval, before returning it to the low table in front of him. "In light of recent events, the severity of the situation and the imminent threat to, not just the elementals, but all the civvies living in San Francisco, we need to move quickly and decisively if we want to prevent a catastrophe."

The other two judges looked thoughtful as they sipped their tea. Judge Sexby's was bubbling by the time it reached his mouth, whereas Judge Nephelus had hardly touched the glass when the surface erupted in serious waves.

"Well, this is certainly a surprise." Finn shook his head as he looked around, trying to figure out what was going on based on the people present. "I thought we had an emergency to deal with, instead it looks like we're going to have a chat?"

"We do have an emergency, believe me. But there are a few things we need to clarify before we can deal with it." Julian sighed and rubbed his temples. "In fact, clarifying what's going on may be the only way to avert a catastrophe."

"What catastrophe are you talking about?" Ty's fists balled and he looked like he was about to jump up from his chair.

Finn grinned. His lover was a man of action.

"There's a tropical storm forming near Isla Socorro, just west of the coast of Mexico. It looks like it will quickly grow into a hurricane and it is heading our way." Julian sighed. "That as such isn't so unusual, and the human tracking services aren't predicting a problem with the storm they've called Celia. But what has us worried are the unusual traces of illegal superpowers mixed up with the nascent storm. The Air People in charge of tracking it are saying it's aimed at San Francisco, which seems impossible. They've never been wrong, though, so everyone is in an uproar."

"What can we do?" Ty was definitely about to jump up now.

"We need to prove who's behind it, so that we can stop him. Since I suspect that black superpowers are involved, we'll need the full approval of the Superpowers court system." Julian sighed. "I thought it was going to be an impossibly long procedure and feared the worst, but once I had presented the evidence available to me, Judge Sexby made me call you back immediately."

"If what you say is true, we're heading for an emergency sitting of the Ultimate Court." Judge Nephelus frowned. "There hasn't been one in over five hundred years, so what makes you think we need one now? Shouldn't we go to the Appeals Court first?"

"That's what we are here to decide." Judge Fathom leant forwards in his seat. "Let me summarise the pertinent facts for you. As you know, we need three judges from three different houses to support the decision for a case to be brought in front of an Ultimate Court. My involvement as a Water Judge is clear, since a water elemental, Louis Hydros, is being accused of causing the problem. The threat, which has been confirmed by independent measurements, could only have been put into place with the help of Air

Power, hence the need for an Air Judge. The third judge is one of our choice and Judge Sexby has kindly agreed to take part, if nobody has any objections."

"I have no problem with the judges chosen for this, believe me." Judge Nephelus waved his hand in dismissal. "I am simply wondering if this is truly the only way."

"You tell me." Judge Fathom shrugged. "The accusations against Louis Hydros are serious and include subversion of justice in the Merrow case and illegal tampering with the Water Court by sending an assassin into a session. He stands accused of two murders of water jurors, canvassing of political support for the purpose of dethroning the Water King and multiple assassination attempts of Finn Garrison, another juror. Need I continue?"

"It seems to me that the conditions for an Ultimate Court case are more than fulfilled." Judge Sexby returned his empty glass to the coffee table. "Add to all this the imminent threat to an entire city, with who knows what kind of consequences, and we have a clear need for immediate action. The only way to stop the hurricane is the combination of all four elemental powers, and we can only do this legally based on an executive order of Ultimate Court level."

"I am aware of this." Judge Nephelus nodded. "Okay, you have my agreement to proceed. But I want a team of prosecutors from all four houses, just in case."

"That will be no problem." Mr. Bainbridge cleared his throat. "I have already obtained the endorsement from the other three partners of Arden, Bainbridge, Chinook and Damek. We are ready to proceed."

"Excellent." Judge Fathom looked around the room as if to check for opposition. "Mr. Garrison, I expect you to be present as a key witness. The same goes for you, Mr. Anglin."

Finn nodded and, from the corner of his eye, saw Ty do the same.

"Mr. Vincent Garrison, you and your charge, Andrew Merrow, will also be called as witnesses, so I would ask you to stand ready." Judge Fathom waited for Finn's father to nod. "Amadis, you will be in charge of transporting Mr. Merrow to the court to be established on one of the Seamounts, probably Rodriguez."

"What's the Rodriguez Seamount?" Ty asked.

"An ancient volcanic island lying deep in the ocean off the coast here in California. Of course, it's ancient to the Muggles—" Judge Fathom's face flushed crimson. "I do apologise, I mean civvies. I've been reading the *Harry Potter* books to my grandson, but anyway... To us, it's one of the last bastions of superpowers mystery."

Ty was impressed. A court session deep under the sea in an ancient volcanic island!

"The session will start first thing tomorrow morning, eight a.m. Pacific Standard Time." Judge Fathom seemed to be in total control of the arrangements. "Transportation for the other witnesses and participants will be provided by Marcel Paradis and Christopher Fire, as needed."

Chaos broke out after that. People started talking, taking notes, making calls and rushing off to do their assigned tasks. All Finn wanted to do was sleep, so he took Ty by the hand and pulled him out of the living room. He had hoped for some sleep before tomorrow's ordeal, maybe some TLC while they were alone.

Closing the back door behind them, he and Finn walked over to his temporary home. Once inside, he sagged against the whitewashed, panelled hallway. It didn't feel like his space anymore. The furnished house conveyed a beach atmosphere with its rattan furniture, soft white carpet and off-white walls and ceiling. The TV and sound systems were state of the art, as was the kitchen equipment. The bedroom upstairs had a great view of the beach and the bathroom was all glass walls and sparkling faucets. Maybe it was all too perfect?

"Where's the bedroom?" Ty whispered against his ear as he leaned very close to him. Finn led the way upstairs and they made it into the room Finn had so cherished in his first days in California.

Ty closed and locked the door behind them. He wiggled his eyebrows suggestively. "Sofa looks comfy."

They moved over to it.

"An Ultimate Court case? The first in over five-hundred years?" Ty asked as he flopped down on the sofa, clearly exhausted.

"I didn't even know there was such a thing. And I grew up knowing my superpowers heritage and judicial history. Couldn't really help it with a father like mine." Finn sank into the cushions next to his lover, leaning his aching head back against the sofa.

"And what is it with Rodriguez Seamount?" Ty frowned, but he put his arm around Finn's shoulders and pulled him close until Finn's head settled on his shoulder. He dropped a kiss on the top of Finn's head.

"Well, I learnt that any potential location for an Ultimate Court hearing needs to represent all four elemental superpowers." Finn stifled a yawn. "So, what we are left with, under normal circumstances, are volcanic islands."

Finn smiled when Ty nodded. "Of course. A perfect combination of fire, earth, water and air." Ty grinned. "Not to mention, since they said it's a sunken island, it's uninhabited by humans. I can't wait to see this place. There are so few uninhabited islands left on the planet."

"It does conjure romantic images, doesn't it? I just hope this hearing isn't going to take too long. This tropical storm is going to get stronger the longer we wait. At this rate, it'll be a hurricane before we know it, and that'll be even more difficult to stop." Finn sighed.

"Nothing we can do about it now." Ty pulled him closer until Finn sat on his lap, straddling Ty's body and smiling down at him. Their smouldering gazes reflected their mutual desire.

"Guess not." Finn said, rubbing his ass back and forth across his lover's lap.

"But I know what we can do something about." Ty's eyes twinkled as he ran his hand up and down Finn's shoulders and arms.

Finn shivered in delight and raised himself up for closer contact. The kiss that followed was hot and deep, quickly followed by another. And another. He moaned into Ty's mouth as his lover opened both their pants and took their hard cocks into his large hands. The urgency went up another notch, as if he hadn't come in the shower just a few hours earlier.

Whatever Ty did to him, Finn wanted more. He gripped Ty's shoulders for something to hold on to as he started fucking the tight tunnel of Ty's fist. He loved the feeling of his lover's cock up against his own erection almost as much as having him inside him.

"God, Finn, so hot." Ty looked up at him with eyes glazed with lust.

"Uh-huh." He wasn't going to last long.

With one final thrust he let go and came all over Ty's hand. Still shaking with the aftershocks, he watched Ty follow suit seconds later. He could do this for the rest of his life and never get bored.

Chapter Nine

"No, no, no!"

Ty scrambled up from the sofa where he'd fallen asleep, almost tripping over his pants, which had bunched around his ankles. He could see it was dark outside. Pinpoints of lights from other houses told him it was definitely night. How long had he been asleep?

He heard the shouting continue. It was Vincent Garrison's voice piercing the otherwise quiet house. Ty heard Finn's gentle coaxing tone as he talked but couldn't make out the words. He reached down, picked up his pants and hurriedly dressed. He groped for the light switch and opened the door. Once in the hallway, he could see the house was brightly lit. The shouting came from downstairs.

"Dad," Finn said, obviously trying hard to get through to Vincent, "you can't wear Birkenstocks with that suit."

"Look, Finn, I've agreed to dress in a suit. No more shark fin. I have no Bermuda shorts, so if I must wear a suit, I want comfortable shoes." He sounded like a petulant child.

Ty interrupted. "Vincent, you're so handsome." He couldn't believe how elegant Vincent looked in his black suit and crisp white shirt.

"His competency hearing went very well." Finn grinned at Ty.

"You mean, I missed it? I can't believe it. Why did you let me sleep through it?"

"It was a breeze, especially when they realised *why* I dressed like a shark. Judge Fathom asked if I was crazy, I said I wasn't. He asked me what day it was and what city we were in. I passed with flying colours. I must say though, I kind of miss my fin." Vincent shrugged. "I can give that up, but I refuse to lose the hippie shoes."

"Oh, all right then." Finn's morose gaze drifted to a pair of black dress shoes on top of a designer-label shoe box on a chair beside them. They were stylish, but so not Vincent.

Ty's cell phone rang as he lifted the shoes out to examine them.

"Well, young man," he heard and groaned inwardly. "Dad?"

"When were you going to tell me about this fancy schmancy court hearing of yours?"

"It's not mine, Dad. It's—"

"I expect you to get me a ticket, son. I'll be at your house first thing. Oh, and your Uncle Yancy wants a ticket, too."

Ty became exasperated. "It's a court hearing, Dad, not a baseball game."

"It's the biggest thing to happen to our people since…the Titanic. See you in the morning."

Tickets. *Sheesh.* Uncle Yancy. *Double sheesh.* Uncle Yancy had a few problems. Lots of problems, actually. He'd been cursed by some water witch and had gills, though with his ever-present red scarf, most people never noticed them.

"Ugly shoes, huh?" Vincent asked him.

"Oh, no. Quite the contrary."

"Really?"

"They're Armani. Chicks love 'em."

"Really?" Vincent's eyes lit up and he snatched the shoe Finn held.

Thank you, Finn mouthed. Ty blew back a kiss to him.

All night long, his cell phone rang. Finn's cell phone rang, too. A few close friends from back home in Bermuda, from whom he'd been kept secluded during the trial, all called. Vincent Garrison got calls from long-lost friends and family members, too. All of them, of course, knew about this special hearing and wanted tickets.

"I've never heard of anything like it," Ty said. "Tickets!"

In the end, the three men scored four tickets between them and lost a multitude of friends. Ty was tickled that Finn and Vincent insisted that Ty give them to his father and uncle, his office assistant, Becca, and her pimply boyfriend.

"If you keep her happy, she'll keep you happy," Finn insisted.

"Are you sure about these shoes?" Vincent asked. "Because my feet hurt."

They squeaked, too.

"Maybe you should take them off, Dad." Finn looked worried. "Shoes shouldn't squeak and tomorrow's going to be a long day."

"No, no, no. They're Armani. Chicks love 'em."

Ty and Finn exchanged smiles.

* * * *

All three men had retired for just a few hours' rest, Finn and Ty in his bedroom, Vincent on the sofa bed in the living room. At the crack of dawn, they all rose, strangely excited and energised. Ty called his dad to give him directions to Finn's house and then came a knock on the door.

Christopher and Marcel came in bearing gifts.

"Bad rain's starting," Marcel said, shaking off an umbrella.

That wasn't good news. The bad storm was already starting. Right now, however, the delectable baked goods Chris had brought and Finn's pot of brewing coffee were too irresistible. Who cared about a little rain when there was good stuff to eat and drink?

"What is this muffin flavour?" Finn asked. "It's gooey and sweet and yet so liquid and smooth."

"What does it taste like?" Christopher asked. Ty noticed the glances he and Marcel exchanged.

"You're going to think I'm weird."

"Try me."

Finn took another bite. He seemed to be afraid to reveal his feelings.

"Well," he said finally, "it tastes like childhood. I taste the sun and sea...it's got a lot of sweetness but a dash of salt. It's watery and yet warm and cosy. Like my mom's hugs." He stopped, emotion getting the better of him. He took a deep breath. "Told you I'd sound weird."

Chris reached over and patted his hand. "Perfect! You were perfect! That's exactly what I wanted to create. It's your perfect childhood. These are blancmange breakfast cupcakes and each person who eats them has a different experience."

Vincent clapped his hands together. "I get it! Blancmange is the kind of dessert most people remember from childhood, but frankly most of our mothers didn't really know how to make it. My mother made it very runny and rather sweet. May I try one, please?"

Chris gestured to the basket. "Please. Be my guest." He held up a hand. "That's the other thing. Once they leave the cupcake pan, they can't be handled by anyone other than the person who eats them, because they are very sensitive cakes and take on the dreams and wishes of all who touch them. In the bakery, we handle them only with wooden tongs and we encourage people who buy them to do the same."

They all took a cupcake. Ty was surprised when his tasted like eggs and bacon and...holy moly, warm grits with butter and grape juice.

"Those were my favourite things when I was a kid." Ty couldn't believe it. His second cupcake was as delightful, sensorial and satisfying as the first.

"This is better than psychotherapy." Marcel licked his lips. "I taste liquorice and raspberries... mmm...and honey, too."

"I'm worried," Vincent proclaimed, taking a delicate nibble. "I was a rather revolting child. I enjoyed eating things like dirt." He swallowed a bite. "Oh, dear...it does bring back memories." He laughed, revealing dirt-stained teeth.

The others laughed. Outside, they heard a crackle of thunder, but inside, eating childhood cakes, it felt safe, warm and oh, so happy.

"You have a winner here," Finn told Christopher, who beamed at Marcel.

"That's what my husband tells me."

* * * *

Ty's father and Vincent hit it off the second they met. Ty couldn't believe his father was wearing a kilt.

"It's my one chance to dress up," his father insisted.

Uncle Yancy arrived swathed in neck scarves, carrying a picnic basket, binoculars and a seat cushion. Introductions made, they had seconds to spare before boarding a bus filled with other Water Folk, bound for some secret destination.

Vincent and Tyros Senior never stopped talking. Ty and Finn exchanged smiles. Christopher and Easter Sunrise paraded up and down the bus, passing out blancmange and cupcakes samples. Marcel kept a doting gaze on Christopher, seemed oblivious as he held an animated conversation with Uncle Yancy.

Those on board the bus soon found themselves heading under the Golden Gate Bridge, past a small homeless community whose inhabitants sat up to watch the spectacle of a bus disappearing underwater. Ty turned around and noticed one homeless man rubbing his eyes, staring in disbelief.

Their bus hovered for a few moments — a couple of buses were ahead of them and more behind — then suddenly dipped down. What looked like a subway opened up and as quickly as they'd entered the sea, they went beneath it.

"What's happening?" somebody asked when they plunged into floating darkness. The bus lights had gone out but the driver announced on a loudspeaker that they would soon be in the court system.

Seconds later, they arrived at a dimly-lit passageway and came to a stop.

Security guards ushered the riders through three different security checkpoints, and then, amazingly, they entered the most lavish courtroom Ty had ever seen.

As the newcomers arrived, a sudden hush fell over those assembled in one of the most exclusive and rare places ever created by the superpowers. Tension crackled in the air as Ty and Finn entered. Conversation came and went in waves.

A bailiff led Finn to a chair on the left side of the room.

"I'll be right back." Ty touched his lover's shoulder, not liking the stiffness he sensed in Finn. Ty wanted to get the lay of the land before he sat down. He made his way around the court, keeping a watchful eye on the attendees. His eyes watered, making him sniff. The odour of moth balls permeated the proceedings.

It was such a hallowed event that the lucky Water House members who'd scored tickets in a last-minute lottery—all proceeds benefitting the preservation of local estuaries—had come attired in what looked to be their best evening wear. One old dear even wore her wedding dress. Another wore a ball gown that had seen better days, but still, the cut-glass sequins stitched to it caught light and movement that bounced off the dress in little rainbow prisms. God knew how long she'd kept the thing in storage.

Ty caught a few people near her shaking their heads as if to exorcise the hold that the rainbows held. He was surprised to see a few of the jurors from the Kennedy and other trials sitting with the spectators. Some of them looked cheesed-off about it. Ty was about to return to Finn, when he spotted Daine and Phillip arriving.

"You're shaking," Ty told Phillip.

"We had a pretty harrowing flash-transport here. Not worth mentioning. Oh, boy…what a zoo!" He rushed past, Daine on his tail. Daine gave Ty a finger wave and Ty waved back.

A bouncy, perky brunette with sparkling blue eyes, a ton of energy and an engaging grin caught up with them. Becca. Ty had seen little of her, since they worked mostly by phone and email, but she was prettier than he remembered. He introduced her to Finn. They seemed to get along the second they met. Behind her stood the tall, gangly, pimply blond guy. Man, his pimples were creepier in the flesh than in photographs.

Ty couldn't talk long since he was working. All of this activity rattled him more than a little. He may have been a Water Marshal, but the excessive use of superpowers over the last few days had made him realise he preferred them to be less conspicuous. He felt more protective than ever of his lover and his sense of threat sparked as he took in the confines of the courthouse.

The court room itself contained an odd mix between the three powers represented in this case and apparently adapted itself to those powers that were using it at any one time. The bench up front seated three judges instead of one. There was no jury present, but both the prosecution and the defence were positioned as in any traditional court room. The space for witnesses, spectators and other interested parties seemed especially cramped, thanks to the extra benches brought in to accommodate the seating frenzy.

The sandy floor felt wet and soft, thanks to the occasional wave. The transparent walls let in different views from the outside world. Last time Ty had been in the Water Court, the view had been the underwater local sea life. This time, the view was somehow more dramatic with its bright coral beds, gigantic schools of fish and giant sharks...and it all seemed more predatory than before. The view extended up, revealing a sunny day — a nice contrast with the earlier rain. The sky was clear enough to afford a view of Mount St. Helens in the distance. He was certain he could see smoke drifting from the active crater.

The court itself, being situated on the low-lying lava plain in the eastern half of the three-mile long undersea island, gave an extra theatrical tinge to the events. Chinstrap penguins were the only current inhabitants, but they didn't seem to mind their visitors in the least. They waddled and swam, taking off as soon as some sharks appeared.

High above them, there appeared to be no roof, in deference to the Air Elementals. Indeed, the whole space felt very light and airy. The floor felt warm — whether due to the nearby active volcano or as a result of the Fire Elementals' presence, Ty wasn't sure. Small flames danced across the glass walls, providing interesting light effects.

"This court will come to order." Judge Fathom banged the gavel three times. All talking stopped. Ty rushed to take his seat beside Finn. On Finn's other side, Vincent gave him a thumbs-up. As he leaned across to do so, his shoes squeaked. Vincent winced.

"We are here to hear the case of Superpowers, represented by the firm of Arden, Bainbridge, Chinook and Damek, versus Louis Hydros, represented by Robert Hydros." Judge Fathom intoned. He nodded at the respective lawyers as he introduced them.

Louis Hydros was an unimpressive man of medium height, with flowing dark hair and deep green eyes. He wore a dark grey suit and what looked to be a permanent scowl, judging by the deep ridges on his forehead.

"My brother was the only lawyer willing to defend me on such short notice, Your Honour." Louis Hydros looked both smug and defensive.

"What are you saying, exactly?" the judge asked.

"Nuffink." Louis Hydros sounded like a Cockney slob. Ty had the feeling somebody had done their best to clean the guy up for his court appearance, but he still talked like a yahoo. Ty's gaze slid over to the brother. Ty hadn't been impressed with Robert Hydros from day one. He wouldn't have inspired confidence in Ty if he were on trial for his life. Not at all. He looked like a Hobbit with his ill-fitting suit, wild hair and spectacularly ugly teeth.

"Your Honour." Phillip Sedgwick held up his hand. "May I address the court?"

All three judges nodded. It was clear they all liked Phillip.

Phillip moved to the desk with a microphone that had apparently been erected for this purpose.

"Your Honour, in view of the fact that Mr. Robert Hydros was working for the defence in the Kennedy trial, it would seem that his representation of his brother is a huge conflict of interest since it is apparent that both men were involved in framing Mr. Kennedy for a crime he didn't commit."

The courtroom observers erupted in a burst of chatter.

"Silence!" the Fire Court justice, Judge Sexby, roared.

The crowd stopped.

Ty noticed little flames licking across the back of Judge Sexby's chair. The bailiff beside him kept jumping back. Probably a good idea.

"Your Honour, I have documents here signed by all four partners of the law firm of Arden, Bainbridge, Chinook and Damek, releasing Robert Hydros from their employment. I also have a subpoena here in which he is being charged with malicious superpowers crimes."

He held up a silver envelope. A gasp escaped a few court watchers.

"In view of the nature of these charges, I informed Mr. Louis Hydros if he chose to engage his brother as his attorney—"

"Your Honour, I told you I couldn't find annuver attorney."

"Mr. Hydros, be quiet," Judge Fathom warned.

"As I was saying, I advised him he would not be able to appeal the court's decision, but he insisted on his right to a speedy trial, and since the three justices present today were busy with this case, I travelled to meet Justice Fox Darwyn, one of the Earth Court judges, and he has signed the defendant's petition for the attorney of his choice."

Wow, Phillip had been busy and probably up all night.

A bailiff collected the envelope. A silver envelope was considered especially bad in the court system. It was usually seen in murder cases…and this one had a few. It was rare and its presence in a case usually signified bad news for the defendant.

"And where is Judge Darwyn?" Fathom asked.

"Indonesia, Your Honour. He is handling a number of earthquake cases and apologises for his inability to be here in person, but he is willing to participate via satellite connection for the final deliberation. He is able to hear everything via phone right now."

"Excellent. Well done," Judge Fathom responded. "Let the record show that Mr. Louis Hydros has been advised of his rights and has chosen his attorney of record."

The courtroom watchers started mumbling again.

A bang of the gavel stopped them.

"As you all know, proceedings in the Ultimate Court are simplified and, in phase one, resemble those of a hearing," Judge Fathom continued. "There is no jury to be impressed by any razzle-dazzle...and the legal expertise of those present is presumed high enough to allow us to focus on the facts, rather than legal procedures."

He gave several people around the room harsh looks.

"Does that mean we don't get to buy peanuts?" the lady in the wedding dress asked. Half the courtroom laughed. The other half began to scarf down whatever snacks they'd sneaked into the proceedings in case they were confiscated. Ty could smell a hamburger. He was sure of it.

"No, Ma," Ty heard a man saying. "This isn't a theatre. It's open court."

"Is it?" The old lady looked astonished.

Judge Fathom glared, but continued. "Once we are ready to proceed to phase two, legal arguments will be made and heard, before we move to phase three, which consists of sentencing." Judge Fathom leaned back. "Mr. Bainbridge, we are ready to hear your opening arguments."

Phillip sat down and Mr. Bainbridge got up from his seat, shuffling a few papers. He took them with him as he approached the speaker's console to the right of the bench.

"We are here to prove that Mr. Louis Hydros is a superpowers criminal of the highest degree. We will show that he was not only behind the two juror deaths in the Kennedy trial but also no less than three attempts on Finn Garrison's life. Since Mr. Garrison was also a juror in that trial, this is a serious offence against the legal system. We further accuse Mr. Louis Hydros of setting up Mr. Kennedy for the murders he allegedly committed. We will also show that he was guilty of Mr. Kennedy's transformation into a sea monster and the unjust conviction of Andrew Merrow. Furthermore, there are several counts of illegal political activity, including bribery of officials, incitement to riot and tampering with votes at both the local and regional levels of Water Power elections."

Mr. Bainbridge left the speaker's console and returned to the prosecution's table. Robert Hydros took his place.

"This case is political, and should not be tried in this forum." Robert Hydros shook his fist in the air. "It's a plot by the saltwater establishment to suppress free thought and continue the unjust discrimination of freshwater people. We will not stand for it."

"Yeah!" his stupid brother echoed. "What he said!"

Ty stared at him. This was a criminal mastermind?

"Mr. Hydros, this is not the time for political statements. And it is not your choice which forum decides your brother's fate." Judge Fathom frowned. "Do you not wish to take this opportunity to let the judges know your point of view? You do realise that your brother will be stripped of his powers if found guilty of any one of these charges? The punishment might be worse if we find him guilty of more than one."

"This is a political witch hunt." Robert Hydros nodded as if to confirm this to himself.

"Very well." Judge Fathom visually checked with the two other judges but they both nodded, so he turned back to the prosecution's table. "Mr. Bainbridge, you may proceed."

"Shit, the Kennedy trial *was* a set-up," Ty whispered to Finn.

While finally getting confirmation for his suspicion that there was something wrong with the Kennedy trial, the thought that someone was powerful enough to mess with the superpowers legal system to this degree was scary.

"Had to be." Finn grimaced. "Can't believe the Merrow case and probably my father's competency hearing are also connected to Louis Hydros. Something's off here. I just can't put my finger on it."

Robert Hydros glared at Mr. Bainbridge as they exchanged places, but Mr. Bainbridge just nodded respectfully and took up his place at the front of the room. This time, he'd taken a stack of notes with him.

"The Merrow case, as old and closed as it may seem, is the key to everything in the Kennedy trial." Mr. Bainbridge looked up from his notes. "Magenta Merrow, who works at Fabulous Cupcakes, was one of the people interviewed when my team looked for explanations as to why Finn Garrison's life kept being threatened. Surprisingly, she not only admitted to passing the information about Finn Garrison's respective locations to Louis Hydros, she also asked the superpowers police to put her into protective custody and requested to talk to Water Detective Julian Narragan."

Ty's eyes widened as he stared at the unassuming looking woman in the audience. He remembered her from his first visit to Fabulous Cupcakes. Only the slight silvery hue around her blonde hair gave away her identity as a Merrow.

"Why would she do that?" Judge Fathom raised his eyebrows and the waves on the floor got a little more agitated. "And shouldn't she have been arrested? Giving away Mr. Garrision's location to potential assassins was illegal activity."

Mr. Bainbridge looked unperturbed. "I would like to call Mr. Julian Narragan as a witness."

Julian walked up to a second console and looked at Mr. Bainbridge.

"Will you please explain to the court why you didn't arrest Magenta Merrow once you had secured her in custody?" Judge Fathom started taking notes, as did his two colleagues.

"I would have arrested her, if she hadn't told me what she did." Julian glanced at Magenta, who sat in the front row.

Bainbridge cleared his throat. "Why don't you tell the court what you revealed to me? You can trust them to treat your information with care."

"Even Vincent Garrison?" Magenta's bright blue eyes adopted a silver hue, a sign of her agitation. "He's my twin brother's gaoler. I don't see how I can trust him."

Vincent's shoes squeaked as he leaned towards her. "I don't see myself as his gaoler...more like his special friend."

Finn nodded vigorously. "My father dressed as a shark for Andrew. He let people think he was crazy, all to make your brother feel comfortable and safe."

"I've kept Andrew safe." Vincent reached out to Magenta and, very hesitantly, she leant forwards and put her hand in his. Something transpired between them...some frisson of attraction. "I was the only one to think him innocent, so I was entrusted with his care."

"You know where he is?" A second woman, a dark-haired beauty, had tears in her eyes.

"Yes, I do, Gladys." Vincent smiled at her. "Look outside."

The audience let loose a collective gasp. Andrew Merrow had swum over to the windows, surrounded by schools of adoring fish. He was such a majestic sight, some people began to cry. Magenta and Gladys threw their arms around one another, weeping.

"Oh, he's beautiful!" the old lady in the wedding dress said, clasping her hands to her face. Arnold" — she elbowed the man beside her — "this is better than *Wicked!*"

"Oh, Andrew! I never left you!" Gladys shouted. "It was all lies. It was him. He kidnapped me!" She pointed a shaky finger at Louis Hydros who rolled his eyes.

The court erupted into bedlam.

"Who is Gladys?" Finn asked his father as the judge banged for order.

"Andrew Merrow's human wife." Vincent still held Magenta's hand. Even though she hugged Gladys and waved at her brother, she held on to his hand too.

"Isn't he handsome?" Magenta kept asking anyone who'd listen.

"Me?" Vincent's voice came out in another squeak. He reddened when it became apparent she was referring to her brother.

She seemed as reluctant to let go of Vincent's hand as he was to release hers. They were forced to relinquish their grips. The judge bashed his gavel. Andrew swam away from the window and the trial continued. Vincent leant forwards in his chair and said sotto voce to Finn, "I didn't know where Gladys was. In fact, nobody did. Louis planted the rumour she'd gotten tired of waiting and ran off with another man. None of us knew she'd been kidnapped."

"Kidnapped!" Several women gasped.

"Yes." Vincent nodded. "Otherwise she would have been allowed to visit Andrew a long time ago...and my dear friend Andrew would not have felt so alone."

Bainbridge spoke. "We'll get to that in a minute."

"I wouldn't say kidnapped, exactly," Louis interjected. His brother put a hand on the criminal's arm but other than that, Robert was doing a bang-up job of letting the formal charges against Louis unspool like a bad movie.

Julian folded his hands and relaxed. "If anyone is going to understand anything, we need to begin at the beginning. Magenta, please, you should go first."

In a halting voice, clearly still hesitant about this idea of telling everyone what had happened, Magenta took the stand and revealed how she had come to San Francisco to find out who was behind her brother's conviction. She'd become particularly curious about the whole thing when Gladys suddenly vanished during her husband's trial. She didn't believe Gladys had done so voluntarily.

"In spite of all I heard, I knew Gladys loved my brother. Some merfolk and humans belong together."

She gave Vincent a significant look and shook her head. As she spoke, waves of silver emerged and the plain duckling of a woman revealed her mermaid beauty. "I was worried," she said, with a shrug. "I had a feeling the Kennedy trial and my brother's trial were connected. I didn't tell Andrew what I was doing. I knew he wouldn't let me continue. Then, when the court moved him and I heard he was in a special water prison, I knew I had to act to prove his innocence."

Ty stole a glance at Vincent. He looked like he'd been hit by the love truck. *Oh, boy.*

"Louis Hydros found out I was digging for information via his brother Robert." She grimaced. "I pretended to like him."

Several people laughed.

She tossed her head again. "He threatened to kill Andrew and Gladys, whom he had imprisoned, if I didn't help him by revealing what Finn was up to. He said..." Her voice faltered. "He said..."

Vincent rushed over to her on squeaky feet. "Bailiff! Bring Magenta Merrow some water."

A bailiff complied. Vincent stood, patting the woman's shoulder as she sipped. Once she had composed herself again, he hobbled back to his seat.

Magenta continued. "He threatened to kill my family. He said he'd kill us and sell us as mer-meat. I don't need to tell you what we'd fetch on the black market."

People started muttering. The very idea of selling sacred creatures as food was appalling.

Ty caught a glimpse out of the corner of his eye of Vincent reaching into his briefcase and extracting his Birkenstocks. He let out an audible *aahh* as he changed shoes.

Probably mermaids dug Birkenstocks. Ty couldn't resist smiling as Vincent and Magenta kept eyeballing one another.

"Can I have your shoes?" Louis leaned across his brother to ask Vincent.

"Can *I* have your shoes?" asked an elderly man having obvious wardrobe and denture issues. Vincent bent, picked up the shoes and turned them over to the old man, who smiled. Louis sneered.

"Gentlemen!" Judge Fathom boomed.

Magenta continued. "I didn't understand why he wanted to know until I heard about the attempts on your life." She had tears in her eyes when she looked at Finn. "But I didn't know what else to do. I couldn't let that bastard harm Gladys and the children, nor Andrew. When Easter Sunrise figured out what was going on, she suggested I get help. I felt like I had no choice anymore, so I did. Julian was the first person I knew I could trust because he was also looking for your assassin."

"I understand." Finn nodded.

"And why was Louis so keen on killing Finn?" Ty was confused.

"That's where it becomes interesting." Julian's eyes shone with the enthusiasm of a detective about to solve a major mystery.

"I'm glad you're so fascinated." Ty glared at Julian.

"It's okay." Finn moved to take Ty's hand then seemed to remember where they were. "Nobody succeeded in killing me, and Julian here is about to solve the mystery, so we should all be grateful he's so good at his job. There's nothing wrong with him enjoying it as well."

"Humph." Ty wasn't convinced, but waved at Julian to continue.

"Louis wants Finn dead because he's the only remaining juror who can see Kennedy and his reactions to what is going on...*and* the only one powerful enough to figure out what *really* happened to Kennedy."

Julian shrugged. "He may not have done it so far, but Louis was clearly afraid that exposure to the facts of the case would lead Finn to the only possible conclusion."

"Which is?" Finn still didn't see what that might be. He hated to admit it, but Louis Hydros had clearly overestimated his deductive abilities.

"Mr. Kennedy was speaking the truth when he said he was framed. The fact is, he wasn't always a sea monster. He used to be a very attractive waterman, just like his elder brothers, the other royal princes." Julian smiled.

Ty was about to jump out of his skin with impatience. He had no sympathy for Kennedy, but if he'd really been framed, that would change.

"What happened?" Finn moved to the edge of his seat.

"Louis Hydros fell in lust with him. When Mr. Kennedy rejected his advances—"

"I wouldn't say rejected, guv." Louis shook his head.

"Shut up!" Judge Fathom barked. Louis kept his mouth shut as Julian continued.

"Anyway, Louis got upset and attempted to kill him, using the ancient, now forbidden, Water Power of Black Frost. Kennedy was able to fight back enough to survive the attack, but his body changed into that of a monster."

Julian grimaced. "Of course, Louis—being who he is—needed to make sure nobody would believe Mr. Kennedy. He set him up for murder, which would ensure his destruction once he was convicted. The court case would also help him discredit the whole royal family, who now looked as if one of them was a murderous villain. Making it seem as though the royals were trying to mess with the case by murdering a few jurors was just the icing on the cake for him."

"And how do you know all this?" Ty frowned. "So far, you've only told us about talking to Magenta, and I don't see the connection yet."

"Don't you?" Julian's grin was provocative.

Finn looked from Ty to Julian and back again. What was going on?

"You said the Merrow case was the key?" Ty's frown deepened.

Julian's grin got broader.

"Oh. My. God." Ty's eyes widened.

"Now you've got it." Julian reached over and slapped Ty's shoulder like a proud father.

"Got what?" Finn looked ready to strangle Ty.

"Of course, why didn't I see that sooner?" Ty smiled. "Louis Hydros was behind all of it. That's just diabolical. And now he's sending a hurricane infused with supernatural power to destroy all the evidence and everyone involved in the case who could prove he was behind it."

"Exactly." Julian nodded gravely. "And there isn't much we can do about it at all. Stopping a hurricane like that will be almost impossible."

"If it weren't all true, I'd be offended," Louis gloated.

"But how did you make the connection?" Finn ground his teeth trying not to yell.

"Magenta here told me." Julian smiled at the woman who'd become very quiet. "Apparently, Andrew Merrow found out about Mr. Kennedy's transformation and tried to heal the prince. Louis caught him, and since Andrew had to make more than one attempt due to the damage being so severe, Louis was able to arrange it so that the image of a drowning man was projected to the humans driving by. He — or more likely one of his henchmen — killed the woman who tried to save the drowning man once she was at sea. He made sure Andrew wouldn't tell the truth by kidnapping his wife and children."

Ty was still grinning, pleased with himself for having figured it out.

"Okay, so that explains Andrew's problem." Finn looked relieved. "But that doesn't explain why Kennedy made an escape attempt the other day."

"You're right, it doesn't." Julian nodded. "Except, it wasn't an escape attempt."

"No? Why has it been reported as such?" Ty scratched his head.

"Judge Fathom made the decision to keep the general public, not to mention Louis Hydros, in the dark until we were able to understand the whole situation. There were too many missing pieces at the time. Not anymore." Julian sighed. "The so-called escape attempt was actually an attempted kidnapping."

"By Louis Hydros?" Ty felt his hackles rise.

"You got it in one." Julian sat back. "He wanted to further incriminate Mr. Kennedy, make him look guilty."

"He almost succeeded." Ty wanted to feel relieved and relaxed, now that everything had been clarified.

"So you see, Your Honour" — Mr. Bainbridge stood straight and proud — "the Merrow case will also have to be reopened and dismissed."

"I can see the logic of your argument." Judge Fathom looked at his co-judges. "Any other questions, gentlemen?"

They both shook their heads.

"In that case, and in the interest of time, we will retire to deliberate the arguments we have heard. You should all remain here for the time being. We will let you know if we believe we'll need more than a few hours. If this goes to plan, it shouldn't be longer than that."

Judge Fathom rose, nodded at this two colleagues and a pair of vicious-looking gaolers appeared. They dropped water everywhere and smelt like sewers, but most court watchers were as fascinated as they were repelled.

Louis screamed while Robert looked worried. Then two more guards appeared. The two Hydros brothers vanished, along with their smelly sentinels.

"I hope I never do anything bad enough to wind up in Water Prison," the old lady in the wedding dress said, shuddering.

Ty concurred.

He watched the judges disappear into another room through a small door at the back. Ty groaned. He hated waiting. But they had no choice. Meanwhile, the hurricane was gaining strength and they were running out of time.

Chapter Ten

Something bothered Finn. He believed they had the right man, but why had Louis gloated when it was obvious he'd be spending a long, *long* time in prison? Finn watched his father hurrying over to Magenta's side. They smiled and talked. The courtroom watchers were all chatting away excitedly, but Finn became increasingly nervous. He was happy for the old man who'd come a long way in such a short time. He felt his mother would approve of Vincent spending time with such a loyal and apparently loving woman.

Could Louis be so deranged that he took pride in his wrongdoings?

No.

The truth came to him so clearly and suddenly that his next thought was, *Dad, I need help.* As quickly as he thought this, his father turned to him, apparently mid-sentence, a look of shock on his face.

Oh, boy. If I'm wrong, both of us will be getting competency hearings.

His father rushed to his side, looking concerned.

"Finn. I know that expression on your face. Have you had one of your visions?"

"What visions? What's going on?" Ty asked.

"Yes, Dad." Finn nodded.

"A vision? You mean a psychic flash?" Ty stared at him.

"We don't have much time," Finn said. "If the clock strikes twelve, not only will the storm front hit us, but a very dangerous witch will have achieved her goal."

"But it's eleven forty-five," Ty spluttered.

"I know. At midday, her power will set and the storm front will roll in. She will take over the Water House and turn us all into virtual slaves."

"Who will?" Vincent asked. "Which witch?"

"That one." Finn pointed at Magenta.

"Oh, no, son, you can't be right. She's wonderful. She's beautiful. She...she's...oh, Finn, are you sure?"

"Yes, Dad. The real Magenta is right there." He pointed to the woman who was dressed in the ball gown with the prisms of glass. "The fake Magenta's bewitched everyone who knew her. If you notice, rainbow lady was sitting behind Magenta and Gladys, so when Andrew came to the window, he was looking at his sister the whole time. He couldn't hear what was being said. He had no idea the woman in front of her was posing as Magenta. He would have seen her real face, which I can guarantee is hideous. She is a sea hag, after all. Gladys of course is human and couldn't tell that the fake Magenta was a witch."

The three men stared at the real Magenta. There was a strong resemblance to the phony, but she was not as beautiful as the witch. She was older, her hair unkempt...with a dazed appearance, so typical of those who have been bewitched.

"The fake Magenta put the gown on the real one so that anyone who knew her but could possibly see the truth would be blinded by rainbows," Finn said. "With the curse removed, the real Magenta will look young again."

"I'm so proud of you!" Vincent hugged Finn so hard, he thought his dad might break some bones.

"How big is the real sea hag?" Ty asked.

"She's slim but quite violent when provoked. Oh, and her hair is long and wild and she uses it to sting. It's the water version of stinging nettles."

"Oh, fab." Ty looked less than enthusiastic.

"Ask Adamis if he has a Neptune Net."

Ty stared at him.

"There must be one somewhere in the courthouse. They are typically used for aggressive water types, though until this case I know there hasn't been an urgent need for them."

"Consider it done. Finn, we need some big-time help." Ty took off, leaving Finn and Vincent to watch the fake Magenta, who chatted away happily with a few adoring human fans. She never noticed the Garrison men's scrutiny, but now that Finn had seen through her disguise, he saw glimpses of the sea hag she really was.

"She never meant to help me," Finn told his father, unable to hide his bitterness. "She expected me to be killed. She had no interest in the outcome of the trial and neither did the Hydros brothers, because she promised them eternal freedom if they went along with all her wild schemes."

"So that's why Louis acted like a buffoon with that fake Cockney accent and making goo-goo eyes at the men in the crowd."

Finn hadn't noticed the goo-goo eyes, but it didn't surprise him.

"And it's probably the reason why Robert put up so little resistance," his father said. "Barely managed an objection."

Finn nodded.

"That's the legend of the sea hag for you," Vincent murmured. "When they gain power, they make promises, but I've never known one who's been able to fulfil them. Finn, I don't want you to be involved in her arrest. If anything happens to you, son, I will never get over it."

"I'll be okay, Dad." He caught Ty's hand waving from the back of the courtroom.

By unspoken agreement, Adamis—who shot out of nowhere with a gigantic, spidery-looking green net—Finn, Vincent and three bailiffs stormed the area where the fake Magenta held her rapt male audience in her thrall. Too late, she realised what was happening and tried to run. She screamed as the net closed over her now slimy, writhing, pustule-covered sea-green face.

Finn threw himself on her, intoning the Riptide Wrath as Adamis secured the netting.

"Return to sender, this message out of a bottle. Leave no charm, render no harm without delay, this blessed creature, out of destruction's way."

The room erupted in a swirl of flung sand and crashing, icy waves, with millions of spiny crabs appearing out of nowhere and hurling themselves at people. The sea hag's full, true form emerged. A slithery, vile creature, she made people scream, crawling all over one another in their haste to get out of the exploding courtroom.

Vincent rushed over to the real Magenta who collapsed in his arms.

"What's happening?" Gladys shrieked, screaming even louder when a crab landed on her nose.

Water started rising—people slipping, sliding and crashing into one another. Judge Fathom appeared, waving his hand. The courtroom returned to normal, the sea hag spitting sludge at anyone near her.

Adamis and the bailiffs dragged her away.

"There goes my moment of glory," Julian said, looking dejected.

"Oh, no," Finn assured him. "You were wonderful. Without you, she would never have revealed herself. She let her guard slip and I sensed it."

Julian perked immediately. "Really?"

"Yes, really."

In the judge's private chambers, before the small group that had gathered at the judge's request, the sea hag had agreed to avert the storm's path in exchange for her life.

"She will be confined to a Louisiana swamp, under heavy guard, but she seems to be happy with this. She has been told she will rule the marshes and swamps. She's as happy as a lark. What we didn't tell her was that nobody else wanted the job. She's so pleased, she's already promising us we'll see vast improvements to the Stillwater communities. Suddenly, she's like Glenda the Good Witch. She's a weird creature," Judge Fathom said.

Finn was mesmerised by the room, which afforded an unobstructed, incredible view of the ancient, submerged island of Rodriguez Seamount. It looked like a maze of caves and hidden ponds teeming with plant and marine life Finn had never seen before. The colours dazzled the senses.

"We deliberately block this view from the courtroom because it's so distracting, but what a visual splendour, isn't it?" Judge Fathom's face went soft when a big, blubbery creature swam by. Everybody in the room became entranced.

The sea animal looked like some kind of dinosaur with a very long, graceful neck, four fins, and a stubby kind of tail. Her eyes tore at Finn's heart. He knew she was a mama, the way she nudged her baby along, full of pride and love.

He watched the pale stripes across her upper body and tail. Her offspring was an adorable mini-me, swimming beside her. Some ancient stirring called to Finn. He felt Ty's hand sneak into his.

"What is it?" Becca, Ty's assistant asked, her tone breathless.

"She's a Plesiosaur. She's supposed to have been extinct for thousands of years. As you can see, she isn't. Isn't she magnificent?"

The concurring murmur brought a brief smile from Judge Fathom. "You are never to mention what you have seen here," he warned. "There are others like her...and we must protect them for the future generations of superpowers children. It's taken us a long time and much effort, but soon, the underworld will no longer be a myth for children. They'll all get to experience the magic and wonder of King Poseidon's treasures."

With things more or less wrapped up, all the participants could return to their lives. Finn wasn't too unhappy that all the trials were over. The only problem was Mr. Kennedy, whose real name was Prince Charlie Brown.

"He didn't mind the name when he was a kid, but he didn't think it was particularly...sexy as an adult,"

Judge Fathom said. "So, he banned people from using it."

Finn laughed. "That's the reason we weren't allowed to use his real name in the trial? His *vanity* was at stake?"

Vincent chuckled. "Well, son, by all accounts, he was extremely handsome and proud of it...before he was attacked. You're the only one I know who's seen him. How ugly is he in his monster form?"

"Oh, God. He's gross."

Vincent nodded. "Precisely."

Judge Fathom continued. "Andrew Merrow has kindly offered to once more attempt to reverse his hideous transformation. Such powerful application of superpowers will take a man like Andrew and his benevolent powers a long time to help Prince Charlie Brown come back to himself."

Vincent turned to Finn. "Andrew is a free man, but I have offered him the waters of Bermuda as his permanent home."

"That's wonderful!" Finn enthused.

The court seemed satisfied with this arrangement and Judge Fathom asked Finn, Ty and Vincent to stay a little longer. Julian, Bainbridge and the others filed out, grumbling and groaning. They obviously didn't want to miss whatever came next.

Judge Fathom waited until their footsteps receded. "Prince Charlie Brown wants to meet you all and to thank you for your help. He is grateful to you, Vincent, because he knew Andrew Merrow to be a kindly creature who tried to help him. In his beastly form, the prince was prevented from saying much other than to constantly repeat that he was framed. Ty and Finn, he also wants to thank you for going to such lengths, even with all the attacks on Finn, to save him."

"No problem…just doing my job," Ty mumbled. He'd blushed with the words of praise, which Finn found endearing.

Finn smiled, surprised when someone squeezed his arm. It was Becca, Ty's assistant. Beside her stood her skinny, pimply boyfriend, who would have been rather attractive had it not been for the gigantic pustules over his face and neck. He was the quiet sort who never said much but Becca doted on him. Finn tried to remember the guy's name then realised they'd never been introduced.

"Can we stay and meet him? I've never met a real live prince before!" Becca gushed.

Finn gave her permission, suggesting she look busy taking notes in her professional capacity. Finn suspected the judge would like anything he did to be recorded for posterity.

"Me? Notes?" she looked appalled. "I do everything on my iPad."

"Do you have it here?"

"No." She pouted like a little kid. "They wouldn't let me bring anything with me into the courtroom."

"Except candy bars," the pimply boyfriend said.

"Indeed." Finn thought with his poor skin condition, the kid ought to lay off the sweets. Maybe Christopher and Easter Sunrise could whip up a healing concoction for him.

As the judge seemed busy on his phone, Finn took the opportunity to remove a pencil and sheet of paper from the judge's desk. He handed it to Becca, who stared at the pencil as if it was a foreign, possibly dangerous weapon. She held it in her fingers seemingly unaware of how to handle it at all. She

seemed to be weighing it, trying to decide if it were heavy enough to break her hand.

Finn was about to say something, when the judge's private door creaked open again.

In walked a man who was half there and half...not. Half of his face was handsome — drop dead handsome, actually — but the other half was hideous.

Becca let out a squeak.

Finn stared at Prince Charlie Brown. The handsome part he could see smiled at him. The beastly part rolled its eyes and poked his tongue out at everyone.

"He's...he's half a man," Vincent said.

"Half monster," Finn mumbled.

The handsome half looked just like...no. It couldn't be.

"You look like my David!" Becca squawked, the pencil flying from her hand across the room.

"David, say something!"

Prince Charlie Brown looked at David, his face bursting into ecstatic smiles.

"Davy!" He raced over to him, hugging him. They both gushed tears and laughter.

"This is my twin brother, Becca," David said, through his tears.

"*Twin*? You...you're a prince?" Becca's eyes bugged.

"Prince Davy Jones. I've been cursed, too. When the sea hag hit Charlie, she got me as well. The only reason she left me alone afterwards was that I disappeared from sight. I pretended to be a civvie. Best disguise in the world."

"Hiding in plain sight," Vincent murmured. "How clever."

"So...the pustules on your face are a curse?" Ty asked.

Prince Davy Jones nodded.

"We can fix that," Vincent said.

"I don't care about the pimples. I've found a woman who loves me in spite of them." Prince Davy Jones put his arm around Becca. "Don't you, darling?"

"Yeah, yeah…but…um…you mean, we can zap 'em off? Man, I've tried everything."

Prince Davy Jones frowned at her. "You have?"

She looked guilty for a moment. "While you were sleeping, I'd put creams and lotions…they'd look a little better then come back worse. Lately, they've looked like they're getting bigger."

Prince Davy Jones looked hurt. "You put pimple cream on me when I was sleeping?"

"I still love you, David," she said, weakly.

He sighed. "Women!"

The two princes expressed a wish for some time together. Finn thought Becca was gracious about relinquishing her beloved for the evening, in spite of some complaints.

"Tomorrow, I'll pick you up," Prince Davy Jones told her. "We'll go to Fabulous Cupcakes and—"

"Really," Becca huffed. "Should you be thinking about sugar when you've still got these pimples?"

"They have recipes there to conquer the pimples," he said, looking hurt again.

"Oh," she said, the smile back on her face. "Well, by all means, let's go!"

"And then I thought we'd look at some…engagement rings."

Becca's mouth fell open and remained that way as Ty and Finn dragged her out of the courtroom. The underwater island grew dark, the marine life disappearing as they filed out of the courthouse itself.

"All my life, I'll be able to look back and say I experienced paradise," Finn said. He kept thinking about the ancient ocean dinosaur. He had always wanted to pet a dinosaur. When he was a kid, his father had once taken him to the Gulf World Marine Park in Panama beach in Florida. He'd been allowed to pet the stingrays. It had killed him to leave that park, but his father had taken him straight back the next day. He felt bereft again right now.

His father put his arm around his shoulders. "I was just thinking about that day, too," he said.

Finn felt grateful and a little surprised that he still shared this psychic bond with his father.

"Come home soon," his father whispered. "I miss snorkelling with you."

As they boarded the bus that would take them back to the civvie world, Ty touched Finn's hand.

"Where does this leave us?"

Finn smiled. "Together, I hope."

"God, sweetheart, I hope so, too. But how do we do this? I mean, I live here…you live in Bermuda."

"I would be happy to travel back and forth. I can't give up Bermuda but I can't live without you either. What do you think about—"

He couldn't finish asking the question because Ty had lunged at him, covering his face with kisses, making Finn laugh.

The bus plunged into darkness then into the ocean and a few seconds later, took them back to dry land.

For one, swift, sad moment, Finn had a ghastly feeling it was all over, but as everybody climbed out of the bus, Ty took him into his arms.

"I have three whole days before I have to get back to work and of course, I want to spend it with you. If you could be anywhere in the world right now, where would you be?"

"With you."

"Yes, sweetheart, I know. But is there some place you'd really like to go?"

Finn hesitated. "Well, I've always wanted to go to Big Sur and ever since Judge Fathom said he was going to plant the idea we were hiding out there, I've become quite...obsessed."

"Big Sur...really? It's close. We can do it...but, I mean...wouldn't you rather Paris, London or maybe Barcelona?"

"Why? I want to be naked in a bed with you in a room with an ocean view."

Ty's mouth opened and closed, before he swallowed hard.

"You just do it for me, you know that?" He kissed Finn with toe-curling passion until Vincent shouted, "Hey you two, get a room!"

* * * *

That was exactly what they did. The next morning, they dropped Vincent and Magenta at San Francisco International Airport. They were on their way to Bermuda. Magenta had turned out to be a true beauty and seemed to dote on Vincent. She even wore Birkenstocks in solidarity with her new love.

"When are you coming home?" Vincent asked Finn.

"Soon, Dad. As soon as Ty gets some time off, we'll be there."

Ty put his arm around Finn's shoulder. "We're looking forward to one of your amazing Cassava pies...and some beers."

"Done!" Vincent beamed and hugged them both.

Ty saw the woebegone expression on Finn's face and became more determined to take time off so he and Finn could visit Bermuda often. They left the airport arm in arm and drove up the coast like civvies in an open-topped convertible sports car they'd rented. Ty had made all the plans, secretive until the end. He'd had Becca organise everything down to the last detail. She already adored Finn and loved being part of Ty's secret plans. She'd booked them a private house at the Post Ranch Inn at Big Sur.

Ty had salivated over Cliff House just from viewing the virtual tour. All the reviews online said it was the most romantic hotel room in California. It certainly looked it. With its deck suspended over the edge of a cliff, its non-stop panoramic ocean views from every single window, no other structure within walking distance...oh, man, it would be utter, decadent seclusion.

The evenings in this part of the world grew chilly, but that would be no problem thanks to heated floors, wood-burning fireplaces and a sunken hot tub.

As they reached the property, Finn gasped in delight.

"Are we really staying here?"

Ty nodded. Their check-in was brief and as soon as they drove up the cliff road to the house, they took out the picnic baskets Finn had spent all morning packing with Christopher. They'd been conspiring like thieves and Ty couldn't wait to see what delicacies his lover had brought.

He had booked the hotel's restaurant for dinner, but Finn's request that they have dinner in bed proved irresistible. As they unlocked the door and stepped inside, the two men were charmed by the thoughtful service. Candles had been lit, flowers and fruit were in bowls around the large unit. It was their own private paradise.

"Come here," Finn said, putting his arms around Ty. "Thank you for bringing me here. I love this place."

Their kiss quickly turned fierce, their fingers and hands roaming one another's bodies. Finn seemed intent on getting Ty naked. Ty had no problem with that. From outside the window, he saw a falcon soaring, cresting—its wild call signalling freedom. That's what loving Finn did for Ty. It gave him freedom.

"I love you," Finn said. "I've been dying to say that."

"I've been dying to hear it. I love you, too." Ty pulled Finn's clothes from his body, his mouth already in tune with every corner and turn of Finn's muscular body. Naked, they fell onto the plush, velvety bedcover. Ty had no idea how they'd stripped completely, so fast. His hand moved to Finn's cock, but Finn sat up on the bed. In spite of the man's raging erection, he wanted to stop? Arrggh!

"Darling, I have a surprise." Finn scooted off the bed which didn't thrill Ty. He watched his handsome partner open first one, then another picnic basket. He lifted out a small, covered silver dish. "I have something very special for you."

"Yeah, I know. I was just about to partake of it, when you rudely took it away from me."

"Ah…this is something even more special."

Finn and his gorgeous cock returned to the bed with the dish and a small silver spoon. When he lifted the lid, Ty's eyes widened.

"Is that…blancmange?"

Finn nodded happily.

"You got over the Kennedy phobia?"

Finn smiled, the look of a secretive man on his face. "Oh, yes. Now, taste."

Ty swallowed a spoonful of the wonderful, creamy pudding. His head exploded with wonderful images of fucking, Finn...hours and hours of fantastic lovemaking...

In this very room.

"It's sex food," Finn reported, breathless as he spooned more into Ty's mouth. "A new formula for lovers. They say it's not safe to drive for at least eight hours after we eat it."

"I don't plan on driving anywhere," Ty assured him, anxious to be inside his lover now. Finn ate a little blancmange, feeding the last bite to Ty. When Ty threw himself on top of Finn and began kissing and humping him, he had wild images in his brain and knew, just knew, that Finn was seeing the same hot flashes.

He began licking and sucking his way down Finn's body, gobbling his man's sweet cock with abandon. Finn bucked underneath him. He didn't speak, but Finn's words resonated loudly in Ty's head.

"*Fuck me, oh fuck me,*" Finn implored.

Ty hunched down between the man's toned thighs, working on his ass with long, wet tongue strokes, preparing Finn for the fucking Ty knew would likely last all night. He lost all sense of time. All he knew was this man, their mutual desire, and the incredible way they touched each other. When at last he entered Finn, he felt like he'd gone to heaven. He'd entered a beautiful, ancient, underground island. Finn clung to him with his legs and arms. He couldn't get enough of Ty into him.

They fucked one another with equal, hard-hitting strokes. Finn's hard cock lay wedged between their rutting bodies. Finn came first, igniting Ty's own orgasm. Ty came so hard, he saw water creatures swimming by—grain of sands falling on him in his underground vision.

Ty felt Finn taking his hand and leading him, still melded as they were into an underwater grotto.

"*Fuck me on this*," Finn said in Ty's head. He broke away from Ty and hoisted himself up onto the rocky lava ledge so his ass stuck out for Ty's pleasure.

"Oh, man." Ty was aware that Finn had in reality moved out from under him and now lay on his belly, ass in the air, begging to get eaten and fucked again.

"What is this grotto?" he asked Finn, coming out of his beautiful, sexy haze.

"It's a place in Bermuda. I can't wait for you to fuck me there."

"I will. Then, and now." Ty was happy to comply with Finn's need for attention. He moved behind his man's proffered and sexy ass.

One thing was for sure, whatever the hell this delicious thing they'd been eating might be, it wasn't his mother's blancmange...

About the Author

A.J. Llewellyn

A.J. Llewellyn lives in California, but dreams of living in Hawaii. Frequent trips to all the islands, bags of Kona coffee in the fridge and a healthy collection of Hawaiian records keep this writer refueled.

A.J. never lacks inspiration for male/male erotic romances and on the rare occasions this happens, pursues other passions such as collecting books on Hawaiiana, surfing and spending time with friends and animal companions.

A.J. Llewellyn believes that love is a song best sung out loud.

Serena Yates

I'm a night owl who starts writing when everyone else in my time zone is asleep. I've loved reading all my life and spent most of my childhood with my nose buried in a book. Although I always wanted to be a writer, financial independence came first. Twenty-some years and a successful business career later I took some online writing classes and never looked back.

Living and working in seven countries has taught me that there's more than one way to get things done. It has instilled tremendous respect for the many different cultures, beliefs, attitudes and preferences that exist on our planet.

I like exploring those differences in my stories, most of which happen to be romances. My characters have a tendency to want to do their own thing, so I often have to rein them back in. The one thing we all agree on is the desire for a happy ending.

I currently live in the United Kingdom, sharing my house with a vast collection of books. I like reading, travelling, spending time with my nieces and listening to classical music. I have a passion for science and learning new languages.

A.J. Llewellyn and Serena Yates love to hear from readers.

You can find their contact information, website details and author profile page at http://www.total-e-bound.com.

Total-E-Bound Publishing

www.total-e-bound.com

Take a look at our exciting range of literagasmic™
erotic romance titles and discover pure quality
at Total-E-Bound.